ANGELINE

A JIM HAWKINS NOVEL

RICHARD A. YACH

Published by Happy Jack Publishing, LLC

Cover design by Tina Lampe

ISBN: 978-1-944104-31-3

The Jim Hawkins Series

THE DESTINY OF JIM HAWKINS

Whatever happened to Jim Hawkins of Treasure Island after he returned to England with Captain Flint's treasure chest of gold?

Rather than choose the safe path, managing an inn with his mother, Jim opts for the adventures of a medical career in Bristol.

Much of what he learns of herbal preparation is from Dr. Robert Livesey and Livian Adams, a beautiful but deaf linen weaver. Undeterred by her disability, their eventual love will last a lifetime.

After his graduation from the London Company of Surgeons, Jim enlists as a surgeon's mate in the Navy. His tour of duty opens his eyes to the slave trade, naval warfare, and smuggling in the Americas.

For a young surgeon, the life-threatening dangers are ever present. If he thought he'd seen enough danger for one lifetime, he was sorely mistaken.

FOR THE LOVE OF LIVIAN

With his sea duty over, Dr. Jim Hawkins marries Livian, his hearing-impaired love and accepts a position at Haslar Royal Naval Hospital in Gosport, England, across the bay from the English Royal Navy shipyard at Portsmouth.

At Haslar Hospital, he tries to maintain his ideals as he confronts a hospital that is more like a prison, full of treachery, deceit, and death.

Life threatening dangers are ever present as Doctor Jim Hawkins attempts to discover a cure for his beautiful wife's deafness, expose the ugly secrets of his colleagues, and defy the culture of slavery that existed in 18th century England.

RAVEN'S REVENGE

Jim's discovery of fraud and attempted slavery at Haslar Hospital earns him a dangerous enemy, Dr. Herman Franks. While at Haslar, Franks and his accomplices kidnap two Jamaican free-women and try to murder Jim. Convicted of kidnapping, Franks vows vengeance on all who had betrayed him, stole from him, or testified against him.

The cruel English prison system of 1772 turns Franks into even more of a vicious killer than he ever was. Fighting for survival after his conviction, Franks frequently changes his name to avoid detection and to secure his freedom. The action in this tale of revenge and bloodlust cranks up the tension and doesn't diminish until the dramatic finish.

These novels can be found in soft cover or eBook at Amazon, Barnes and Noble, and iBooks.

DEDICATION

To Linda: for her inspiration, encouragement, and support.

ACKNOWLEDGMENTS

I want to acknowledge the help I received from readers of early drafts of this novel, including Linda Yach and my editor, Beth Burgmeyer. Without her professionalism, publishing, and editing excellence, this novel could not have been possible.

CHAPTER 1

Around a circle twenty-feet in diameter on the warehouse's dirt floor, six male drummers pounded out a steady, hypnotic rhythm. Each drummer was accompanied by a woman shaking a bean filled gourd with one hand and rattling a handmade tambourine with the other. Synced with the drumbeats, the combination of these crude instruments created a simple Jamaican beat that aroused the primeval needs of a hundred intoxicated "worshipers."

Many danced mildly as the gentle, relaxing music relieved their pain and grief. Some danced more wildly as if they had a demon that needed to be exorcised. For many of the men and women assembled, their response to the ceaseless drumming depended on the amount of hallucinogenic herb-soaked rum that each had ingested.

The mesmerizing slapping of these African-Jamaican gumbe drums continued without pause throughout the late afternoon and into the evening, and helped create an altered, trance-like state among the crowd. These drumbeats were their connection to their ancient African culture and religion. Some members of the crowd murmured African and Jamaican-Creole single words while others cheered with exclamations of joy as they attempted to contact their personal version of a spiritual dimension.

These Jamaican dockworkers, shipbuilders, charwomen, maids, and ordinary laborers were seeking emotional healing at this Sunday assembly. Each of them sought the escapist trance they gladly received from the effects of the salvia hallucinogen herbs that had been mixed with the rum. It was ladled from large common bowls in the middle of the circle next to a small fire, a fire kept small to prevent ignition of remnants of the cotton and tobacco often stored in the warehouse. The line at the bowls was congested as participants slurped up the drug-filled liquid and took a spot back in the circle.

More of the salvia, harvested from the Farlington marshlands area northeast of Portsmouth, was passed around mixed with blunts of tobacco. The harvested drug had its intended effect as the early evening wore on, creating zombie like men and women chanting and thinking they were having an out-of-body experience. The Obeah man had planned the entire ritual.

Known as Sobadu, the Obeah man, well-experienced in herbs, knew the effects of the salvia were short-lived. It produced hallucinations for about thirty minutes where the poor Jamaicans would see things that weren't really there. He expected them to have changes in vision, a visceral body sensation, and radical emotional swings. He expected them to lose contact with reality. It was because of this short lasting high that he had prepared blunts of the drug to reinforce the high through the night.

As the drums kept sounding their deer-skinned thump-a thump thump… thump-a thump thump… thump-a thump thump… two or three Jamaicans yelled out:

> Papa Legba!
> Papa Legba!
> Papa Legba! Oyey Baye Pou Mwen!

Other men yelled from deep within their souls as if they were trying to bridge the ethereal distance between themselves and their ancestral past. Others in the crowd chanted loudly over and over:

Obi-loa- Oh…ANA-LEA-MAH
Obi-loa- Oh…ANA-LEA-MAH
Obi-loa- Oh…ANA-LEA-MAH
Obi-loa- Oh…ANA-LEA-MAH

The laborers were well into an hour of drumming, chanting, and drinking the drug-laced concoction. Watching soberly out of sight as the crowd's chanting raised the emotional temperature in the room, Sobadu and his henchman, Slash, nodded to each other in agreement that the time was right for the Obeah man's grand entrance into the middle of the circle.

Sobadu was a Jamaican around fifty years of age and much taller than the average man. Dressed for his entrance, the Obeah man wore his full costume. He sported a top hat, black tail coat, dark glasses, and cotton plugs in his nostrils, as if to resemble a corpse dressed and prepared for burial in the Obeah Jamaican religious concoction emulating Haitian voodoo practices. His face was crudely painted with white talc so it resembled a skull. He had a pipe in his mouth which he smoked constantly. He mainly smoked tobacco, but every so often during his "show" he would pull up some of the salvia from his coat pocket, light it in his pipe as he circled the room, and blow smoke in someone's face, intensifying the intoxicating effect of the herb as the recipient inhaled it.

Sobadu jumped in the middle of the circle, and with the drums, gourds, and tambourine supplying the background, he yelled as loudly as he could:

Papa Legba!
Papa Legba!
Papa Legba oyey baye pou mwen, ago eh!
Baron Samdi,

Spirit of Obeah, I offer you food and rum.
I offer you incense.
I call on you to grace us with your presence.
Papa Legba! Ayibobo!

Sobadu weaved into the middle of the dirt floor. He moved with great energy, hopping like a giant frog around the interior of the circle, alternating from a crouch position to his full height, springing up close to a participant's eyes, staring for a moment, then laughing viciously. He did this to many as he moved around the circle of men and women closest to the inner ring of the circle. As the crowd inched its way back from the Obeah man, it enlarged the space in which he would perform his Obeah magic.

The shouting and chanting continued. The men and women yelling, shouting, chanting. Sobadu chanted with them, in a pounding rigor of joy, relief and celebration. The din rose to a climax. Sobadu yelled the chant as loud as he could, trying to drown out the rest of the crowd:

Obi-loa- Oh …ANA-LEA-MAH
Obi-loa- Oh …ANA-LEA-MAH
Obi-loa- Oh …ANA-LEA-MAH
Obi-loa- Oh …ANA-LEA-MAH

Sobadu motioned to the drum beaters and tambourine players to stop. The room slowly turned quiet and Sobadu began his speech.

"I am Sobadu the Obeah man with the power to protect everyone from harm or invoke the spirit of Baron Samdi to destroy your enemies!

"I am of African-Ashanti blood. Know this, you who are new to me. I kept Tacky and his Jamaican rebels free from harm with Obeah magic and I protect you now too, enslaved in England!

"You come to me for spiritual guidance. You do not trust the English doctors but come to me for healing herbs. I possess the spirits you need. You have Sobadu to care for you. I have the medicine you want. You can never rely on the English to help you. They only want to abuse you. Trust in me! Trust in the power of Obeah!

"When you were a slave you had no choice but to bear the whip and the club or to escape. Escape! Yes. Many tried only to be caught and hung like a pig. Now you are freemen and women. Yes! Yes! Yes! The English courts have decided that any slave in England is a freeman or free woman! Yes, Here! Not in Jamaica! Oh, no! Not in the colonies, but only here in England. But you can be glad. Now you are free and can rejoice. Chant loudly with me to celebrate this freedom!"

The drums and tambourines took up their beat again as Sobadu danced by himself in the middle of the circle around the small fire. Over and over they chanted:

Obi-loa- Oh...ANA-LEA-MAH
Obi-loa- Oh...ANA-LEA-MAH
Obi-loa- Oh...ANA-LEA-MAH
Obi-loa- Oh...ANA-LEA-MAH

When the spirit moved him, Sobadu once again quieted the music.

"Ha! Ha! Ha! Are you English now? Tell me... Are you African now?... Are you Jamaican now?... What are you? You have your freedom now, but only here in England. What will you do with it? Will you jump on a boat and go back to Jamaica where you would be a slave again? Drummers! Continue!

The drums and gourd shakers resumed their beating as Sobadu ran around the circle and yelled at each of the people on the inner circle. He yelled in their faces, "Are you English now? Are you African? Are you Jamaican? What are you?"

Sobadu's tone of voice heightened as he seemed to demand an answer from each person he stopped in front of. The drums were still beating. People were still chanting, mumbling to themselves and towards the ceiling, turned on by the narcotic-laced rum. They were zombie-like in their hypnotic trance.

He had power over the entranced participants and he knew it. He cultivated this power for the past ten years he'd been in Portsmouth. He gave them some herbal relief and Jamaican Obeah spiritual belief and they brought him rum, food, women, and clothes. He carefully, craftily, carved out an industry in Portsmouth. He had done the same in Jamaica where people believed him and his ancestors who delivered herbal treatments and practiced the cult of Obeah.

"Come to me!" Sobadu yelled. "I can protect you! The world outside is evil and will harm you. I can see the future. For ten years I have given you counsel. I have given you Obeah! Call on your Obeah man to grant your wishes. I alone have the power to summon Baron Samdi to destroy your enemies! To see your future. Your future is now and it is with me!"

Sobadu then led the men and women in a rhythmic chant.

"Are you English?" Sobadu yelled above the drumbeats.

The crowd murmured in scattered unison, "No."

"Louder, I say!... Are you English?!" Sobadu screamed.

The crowd responded louder, "No!"

Sobadu continued in a loud voice, and got a more resounding response with each question. "Are you West Indian?"

Some shouted, "No."

"Are you Jamaican?"

The crowds yelled, "Yes!"

Sobadu continued. "Then to which country do you belong? Are you English?"

"No. No, not English."

Sobadu insulted them with a sneer in his voice, like a ringmaster in a circus. "The English think you are still a slave. Do you want to go back to Jamaica?"

The refrain was loud by now as the emotional fever in the room rose. "No Jamaica!" a man yelled. "I don't want to go back there."

"Then in which country do you belong?" Sobadu yelled. "I

remember Africa. I remember a land where black fought against black. Do you want that? I remember a land of slavery. Oh, yes, I remember Africa where one tribe would enslave another conquered tribe. Sell them to the English, French, Spanish. But it is not home. Am I Ashanti tribe? Oh no. Will they fight the tribe Fante here in England? NO!"

Sobadu answered his own questions. "It does not matter what your tribe was. Who reveals themselves as Jamaicans and also Ashanti? No one. Here there are more African tribes they say. We must know that we are all together despite where we were born or what tribe our ancestors came from! We are all together as one race of black men and women. We are slaves no longer. We must help one another. Black will not fight black in England! We must be free. We must be together. Will you join me? Will you join me? Will you join me?"

The crowd's response was firmer this time despite their entranced state. "Yes!"

Sobadu in full voice asked, "What will you do? Say it loud to bring the spirit of Obeah to us to give us strength."

Papa Legba! Ayibobo!
Papa Legba! Ayibobo!
Papa Legba! Ayibobo!

The crowd chanted along with Sobadu, continuing their harmonic chant for five minutes:

Obi-loa- Oh…ANA-LEA-MAH
Obi-loa- Oh…ANA-LEA-MAH
Obi-loa- Oh…ANA-LEA-MAH

Obeah man chanted along with the crowd in rhythmic cadence. Everyone swayed to the drumbeat. All watching were mesmerized by his seemly out of body behavior in his unworldly costume calling on spirits to be directed through him to help these poor unfortunates, Obeah's neglected spirits.

Sobadu turned toward Slash, his brutal psychopath assistant who was watching Sobadu carefully. Sobadu nodded to him as a signal. Slash was thin and wiry; a smallish, agile man with a nasty disposition. Slash never took any drugs or "medicine" per instructions from Sobadu lest he be intoxicated and not able to do his master's wishes at a moment's notice. For ten years he had been a protector of Sobadu and had been his main, well-paid enforcer.

He had been silently waiting and lurking in the warehouse, observing all the raucous, loud, and intoxicated behavior of Sobadu's crowd. After he saw his sign from Sobadu, he went into the corner of the warehouse and roughly lifted a Jamaican from his knees to his feet. The man had been bound and gagged so he could not cry out. Slash brought him to the middle of the circle and forced him to his knees. Sobadu motioned for the drums and tambourines to stop.

"Many of you know this man. He is called Jonna. Those of you who work on the docks know him. He has become your overseer and many of you have complained to me that he has abused you. Treated you harshly, even used the whip and the club. Is that not so?" With this last question, he yelled it as loud as he could. "Baron Samdi come visit me. I want your blessing for what I'm about to do. Do you want this traitor dead? Not dead? No? Something worse, then?!"

Members of the crowd already riled up to a fever pitch saw Jonna kneeling before them, the fire close to his knees. The Obeah man Sobadu hovered over him, with drum beaters continuing their rhythms with an almost deadly apprehension.

Sobadu bent down to the kneeling Jonna, and with a voice intended to frighten him, he yelled in his ear loud enough for the crowd to hear him over the sound of the drums.

"You… Jonna. You are an overseer! You have beaten, tormented, and abused your fellow Jamaicans who have worked for you. Look in their faces. They want you to pay for your crimes. You have made them feel less than human and have elevated your status at their expense, and pain. They want you to suffer pain for your sins. I have been asked to deliver your punishment. I know you to be a nonbeliever, having given yourself over to the English. You have treated your fellow Jamaican slaves harshly. Are you this man?"

Sobadu sneered down at Jonna and yelled in his ear. Bound and gagged, Jonna couldn't answer back. It was only the frightened look in Jonna's eyes that told Sobadu that he had sent fear into this man's heart.

"You… Jonna are a non-believer in Obeah. I will teach you the strength of Obeah. I will show you and all that are here the power of Obeah over life and death."

Sobadu turned to Slash. "Hold him."

Slash and another did so.

The rest of the intoxicated onlookers grew quiet and could not move a muscle. They were hoping for some retribution to this man. But death? Would Sobadu kill him?

Obeah man drew a vial from one of the two sachets that he had tied to his waist. He reached down and picked up a large sponge that had been given to him by Slash when he entered the area. Sobadu opened the vial and poured a copious amount of oil from the vial onto the sponge, then forcibly rubbed the man's neck, face, and scalp with it.

Sobadu was the only one who knew what the oil was, where it had come from, and what it would do to Jonna. He kept these herbal secrets to himself. Even though Slash had helped him collect the deadly ingredients from the Farlington marshes, Slash had no knowledge of what the final mix was. Slash didn't have the mental capability to comprehend the concept of mixtures and herbal formulas. These Sobadu had learned on the isle of Jamaica from his father and his grandfather.

The poisonous potion was made from squeezing a freshly-killed blue lizard, plus the heart and liver from a dead toad wrapped in a dried sea worm. Sobadu had added an 'itching pea'—an exotic type of vine to the vile mix. All combined into one mixture, they were similar to the toxins from liver and reproductive organs from the Caribbean pufferfish that Sobadu had used a decade ago in Jamaica to put his subject into a low heartbeat coma.

As Sobadu roughly applied it for a minute or so, Jonna slowly became comatose. With a nod from Sobadu, Slash and the other man let Jonna fall to the ground face first. The crowd let out a hushed gasp as Sobadu bent down, rolled Jonna over, and listened to his heartbeat. It was almost negligible.

Sobadu yelled, "Jonna has paid for his sins. All power to Obeah. Say it with me!"

The crowd responded with a yell of relief and confused excitement. There was no shame. No regret. Just an animalistic roar of approval. "All power to Obeah," the crowd shouted!

The drums and tambourines started their music and the crowd started to move slowly then more rapidly in a dance around Jonna's body.

He was motionless for a half hour. Sobadu made the crowd think that Jonna was dead. The crowd was convinced that the power of the Obeah man and his oil caused the death of his victim. But after a passage of time, Sobadu seized the moment and with a nod, quieted the drums and the tambourines, and addressed the crowd once more. He had purposely allowed only a half hour to pass since he didn't want the salvia and rum to wear off. He wanted their overly-sensitized feeling to be swayed by his magic.

"By the power of Baron Samdi and the power of Obeah, I have put this man down as you asked. But Obeah can be merciful to those who believe in him. I will bring Jonna back to us. He will believe in Obeah. He will believe in me and my magic. He will be a changed man."

Sobadu bent over Jonna who was lying on his back. He stealthily covered Jonna's entire body so no one could readily see what he was about to do. Slash quickly helped by pulling Sobadu's coat over his head to help shield him.

Sobadu pulled the second sachet from his waist band, took out his distilled and crystalized shavings of the antlers of the red deer, heavily dampened them with some of the salvia rum mixture from the common bowl, placed it on the opposite side of the sponge that he had used before, and shoved the sponge into Jonna's nostrils and forced him to inhale. The smelling salts from the deer antler shavings had its intended effect. It irritated the nostril membranes and lungs so much so that it triggered a sharp inhalation reflex, bringing in more air and oxygen and increasing his heart rate.

Sobadu had done this before. He was confident that Jonna would be brought back to the living. As Jonna awoke, a great cry came from the crowd. Most were still intoxicated, in a simplistic stupor and were in awe of the power of the Obeah man when Jonna sat up and looked at the crowd around the circle. Gasps went up from the inner circle who had a clear view. They were convinced that Sobadu had the power of life over death.

"The man is neither dead nor alive," exclaimed a bystander.

"He can't speak," said another.

"He has no feeling," shouted another.

"Good for nothing more than ploughing the fields," yelled another.

Jonna spoke as he sat up and swore his allegiance to Sobadu and to all that he commanded since Sobadu had saved his life.

As the crowd chanted, "Sobadu! Sobadu, Sobadu!" Sobadu welcomed Jonna back to life and bade him to report for his job in the morning and plead with his bosses to allow him to accept a job lower in status. He also told him to come and see him two nights hence since he would have a job for him to do that would require his total obedience to the power of Obeah.

Jonna readily accepted and danced with the rest of the crowd until the music stopped late that evening. Sobadu and Slash snuck out the back while the crowd was still chanting.

Sobadu gloated that his Obeah ceremony had been a success as he and Slash made their way from the building. He was proud in his ability to control the black men and women who believed in his witchcraft. He needed their complete compliance. It was all part of his plan.

CHAPTER 2

HASLAR NAVAL HOSPITAL
GOSPORT, ENGLAND

Dominique had only to walk a half mile to the Haslar Hospital graveyard from her home that she owned at Gosport with her daughter, Angeline. It was a cool summer night with a breeze coming off the Solent strait that abutted the naval hospital and its much-used graveyard. Dominique had walked this path and snuck into the graveyard a number of times during the two years she and her daughter had been both slaves and freewomen for the hospital administrator.

Every time she made this short walk in the middle of the night, it was for a specific reason. She would not drift aimlessly among the hundreds of dead buried in the ten-acre site behind the hospital. As she deftly climbed the fence, she was thinking about finding what she needed from a recent shallow burial. That wouldn't be difficult. Sailors and soldiers were dumped off at Haslar every month and many did not survive their wounds.

She wanted something tangible. She had obtained similar fetishes before and she wanted another one tonight.

Dominique knew the graveyard well and knew where the recent dead would be buried. Hospital orderlies didn't plant the poor dead military men deep. The water table from the Solent that was next to the graveyard was too high for six-foot deep plots. Hence, the graves were shallow and could easily be unearthed and she could get what she wanted.

With the summer moon lighting her way, she quietly found a new gravesite and used her hands to cast the loose top layer of dirt away and burrow until she found the coarse linen sheet that covered the body. In her ritual, it was important to use her physical hands rather than some tool to dig for the dead. When she had exposed the linen-wrapped body, she took a sharp kitchen blade that she had carried with her and cut the burial sheet until it revealed the arm of the dead sailor. She abruptly pulled it up from the sheet through the dirt.

She didn't stare long at the arm but held it while she used the knife to firmly cut through the wrist between the carpals and the radius bones, letting the hand drop to the earth as she finished. No blood dripped since the life had gone out of the dead man at least two days earlier.

She didn't waste a moment, but wrapped the hand along with a small amount of dirt inside a rag which she had drawn from her waistband, wiped the knife as best she could, and firmly stuffed the handless arm back into the ground. Then she brushed dirt back onto the grave, a grave that the indifferent guards and hospital administrators would never revisit.

Once at the fence, Dominique looked both ways to see if one of the sentries that slovenly and often drunkenly patrolled the circumference of Haslar Hospital was actually walking his rounds. When she spotted none, she got over the fence and walked carefully back to her house.

It was two in the morning when Dominique had her shrine assembled. The dead man's hand was the main object in her array of fetishes, all of which had special meaning for Dominique's worship of Myal. She believed each had supernatural powers, a connection to the otherworld. Even though the newly acquired hand was the centerpiece, the other objects had power as well. The salt, wax, aromatic oils, candles all had meaning for her. Dominique had carried the worship of Myal in her heart since she had been in Jamaica and often prayed to Myal, the counter belief to the African-Jamaican practice of Obeah.

The worship of Myal helped Dominique remember her roots. Although she and Angeline had been in England three years—partly as slaves to Duncan the hospital administrator and now as free women—she never wanted to forget her Jamaican background, hard and brutal though it had been.

The worship of Myal was part paganism and part Christian. Rooted in their Ashanti West African witchcraft, many slaves brought the worship of Myal and Obeah with them to Jamaica along with priests and shamans who mixed worship rituals with herbal medicines and poisons.

Obeah practitioners generally used Obeah rituals for dangerous sorcery, and Myal was most often employed for healing and to counteract evil, although the two were often blurred together. Practitioners of both sides of this belief system were well versed in poisons and organically deadly substances. Dominique's mother had been a strict Myal woman who had taught Dominique everything about Jamaican flowers and herbs—those potentially helpful and those potentially harmful.

Dominique knelt before her small makeshift altar, ritualistically lit two candles, put some of the oils in a tin plate, and held it suspended above a candle flame so that the room would fill with the sweet smell she associated with Jamaica, her mother, and her Myal. She held the tin plate just long enough over the heat for the oils to send out their pleasant, almost intoxicating smell. The aroma of the fragrant, wispy smoke made her a bit melancholy as she started her prayer to invoke the spirit of Myal. It was a prayer of thankfulness, and a prayer of supplication.

Oh, Myal, where do I belong? I have this baby, this Angeline of mine. No longer a girl but a young woman.

Strong willed she is. Strong and royal like her father, Tacky.

Strong and brave and royal.

Oh Myal, you have given her to me and I thank you.

You have kept us safe on our journey and I thank you.

You have protected us. Thank you.

Angeline is strong and willful. Be kind and protect her.

You have been with us in Jamaica. You have been with us in England. Oh, Myal, where do I belong? I am Jamaican, I am African, yet I am in England. It is not my home. But where is my home?

We will do what you wish.

I have done some things I am not proud of.

Forgive me my sins.

I have done what I have needed to keep my baby and me safe from harm. Forgive me my sins.

I will do what you wish.

Dominique bent over the altar and gently put some of the dirt on the severed hand. She grabbed a rag and put some of the oils on it as well. It was a small ritual, but it had meaning. She continued her prayer.

Myal,

You are my church. No stained glass. No pointy steeples.

There is no organ music.

But there is no life without Myal.

You are the church.

To you I bow.

There is but me and Angeline.

Silent I will not be.

I will pray to you to keep us safe.

I pray for your kindness.

But if evil befalls us, help me to become a cursing Obeah woman. Those who harm me or my child will fear me and die.

Dominique had just finished her prayers when Angeline appeared at the door to her mother's bedroom. Angeline had been awakened by the sound of her mother's chanting. She quickly identified the smell of the candle smoke. She got up from bed and walked toward the dim candlelight in her mother's room.

When Angeline saw the severed hand and the candles, she couldn't contain herself. "What are you doing, Mother? You told me you were going to stop this pagan ritual!"

Abruptly startled from her reverent mood, Dominique spun around on her knees and faced her daughter. It was obvious that she was not going to let this insult to her and to her Myal go unchallenged. "I have told you it gives me peace."

Angeline walked straight to the small altar, and even though Dominique was still kneeling, bent down, pulled the severed hand from its holder, and shook it in her mom's face. "A severed hand, Mother! Did you go to the graveyard again? Did you rob a grave for this? What kind of paganism is this?"

Dominique's eyes were fierce. "Don't you dare question my belief in Myal. She is the earth mother of sanctuary, blessing, and healing. She has kept you and me safe during these years of slavery. Don't be cruel. Let me have my peace, Angeline. Let it alone."

"I can't. It's grotesque. It has no place here in England. If anyone saw this, you would be branded a witch, accused of sorcery and heaven knows what else. You could be hanged. Don't you see that?"

"I am not a witch. I pray to the goddess of healing and safety. Myal has kept us safe. We are alive today. We prosper. It is the spirit of Myal that guides us."

"You are in England," continued Angeline, not willing to give into her mother's arguments as much as she might have when she was younger. "You are not in Jamaica. You are not on a sugar cane plantation. You are not in the jungles anymore. Not in the hill country."

"No. We are not. In Jamaica when I was with your father, Tacky, Myal kept us safe even during the massacres. When we ran into the Santa Maria mountains, Myal kept us safe. I will not deny the power of the earth mother to continue her protection."

"That's superstitious nonsense, Mother. I can't accept it. We make our own fate," barked Angeline in defiance. "We have free will under the blessings of Christ."

Dominique shook her head. "What's the difference? I see none. No, of course you can't believe in Myal. I kept you from it. You were schooled in Christianity by the Stewarts after they bought us in Santa Maria. I allowed it. I didn't fight it, did I? Well, did I? Did I?"

"No. You didn't."

"When we worked in the Stewart's Jamaican plantation house, it was my wish that you would be better off than me. It was me that begged Mrs. Stewart to teach you in the English ways with the English religion. Don't be angry with me. You can read and write and do math because I allowed it."

"You learned to read and write as well," responded Angeline, trying to make an argument she would never win.

"You are much better than I am at both and much more. But you must understand that you were taught their religion because I allowed it. Now, don't throw it in my face. I don't want to change. It was Myal that kept us safe. When master Stewart took us to England and had to sell us, I begged him to sell us as household servants so we had a roof over our heads and food on the table. He made sure we were sold in England as household servants. Myal did that for us. In Dr. Duncan's home at Haslar Hospital we cooked, we cleaned, and even put him to bed when his opium dreams put him to sleep. We were safe. So don't you sass me or blame Myal. She is very powerful. She kept us safe."

Angeline let out a frustrated sigh. She needed her mother to see how dangerous her beliefs were. "Christianity is the religion in

England. We must conform. You must conform. You don't want to be arrested."

Dominique no longer looked like she wanted to have this conversation, but Angeline persisted. "What would Eli Williams think if he knew you were secretly stealing body parts from his hospital graveyard? You have to stop this. We have his linen business. We are prospering. We are independent. We are no longer slaves. We can't afford to lose Eli's good will. It's in Galatians, Mother: *as you sow, so shall you reap*."

"That's enough bible quotes for tonight," said Dominique. "Go back to bed."

"Not just yet," demanded Angeline. "Sometimes when I look at you, I'm not sure that I am your daughter."

"How dare you say that? I have kept you safe all these years."

"I don't look like you, Mother. My skin is so much darker than yours."

"You are my daughter. I bore you. I gave birth to you. You came from my womb, Angeline. But you are also your father's child. He was much darker than me. You have his royal blood. And his temper."

Angeline had found out something that she had never known before. Dominique rarely talked to Angeline about Tacky, the rebel leader. "Some things you never know until you ask," said Angeline, as she calmed down and once again felt sympathy for her mother who had endured so much to keep them safe. "I'm sorry for what I said. I'll leave you alone now. Please douse the candle before you sleep so you don't inhale the fumes."

As Angeline went back to bed, she thought about her mother— all she'd been through before and after Angeline was born.

Dominique had endured slavery for ten years on a plantation in Jamaica. Light-skinned, she had the high cheekbones and pleasant features that Tacky had been attracted to. She had been one of Tacky's mistresses when she gave birth to Angeline. When Tacky started his vicious, deadly, yet short-lived slave rebellion in 1760, he insisted that Dominique and four-year-old Angeline head north to the port of Santa Maria, where they might be able to escape slavery. It didn't happen. Captured, Dominique could have been lawfully hung, but a magistrate took pity on her since she had a small child and gave her over to the slave traders.

At Santa Maria, she and Angeline were resold to Zachary and Abigail Stewart. The couple was kind enough to bring the young mother and her daughter into their house as servants.

Strict Calvinists, the Scottish couple took pity on Dominique. She was a young woman at the time, in her early twenties. Once they had been told what had happened during the rebellion, they took the two women into their household. Over the next nine years, Abigail Stewart taught Angeline how to read and write, and she showed Mrs. Stewart that she could be a very bright student when she wanted to be.

The Stewarts had used the two women—both with light, gentle facial characteristics—as house maids and thus spared them the rigors of sugar cane planting, harvesting, and curing. Since he was a religious man, Zachary Stewart was upright, yet strict in his treatment of the two women who tended to his and Abigail's needs.

There was also bible teaching. Angeline had her own small room in the plantation estate house, and read the bible as instructed every night. Abigail Stewart had a mission to take a young girl with no preconceived notions of what religion would be and mold her ideas slowly and carefully and point them toward a Christian God and a belief in Jesus Christ as Savior of all mankind.

When Zachary and Abigail sold their plantation, moved to Portsmouth and eventually back to Scotland, they sold the two women as slaves.

◆ ◆ ◆

The next morning after their confrontation, Angeline and her mother didn't speak over their morning oatmeal but went straight to the weaving shed and got to work. Both knew that they had to meet their commitments to Haslar Hospital by delivering cotton sheets every week. They could not allow their differences to get in the way of the production quota. They needed to work the loom ten hours a day, six days a week, in order to make the number of sheets that Eli Williams required. If they didn't fulfill their end of the agreement, someone else was all too eager to take their business from them.

That production of cotton sheets to Haslar Hospital had been arranged by Dr. Jim Hawkins and his wife, Livian, when they moved to Bristol. The two women had been extremely lucky in a number of ways. They had been rescued by Dr. Jim Hawkins and his colleague Dr. David Mclaughlin when another physician, the dark and sinister Dr. Herman Franks had tried to sell them on the Isle of Cowes. But even after that scare, Dr. Hawkins had forced Duncan, the hospital administrator, to sign documents freeing them from slavery.

When Dr. Hawkins and Livian and Mclaughlin moved to Bristol, Hawkins had sold the loom to the women so they could earn a very good living selling cotton sheets to Eli Williams at Haslar Hospital. And beyond that, it was a stroke of tremendous good fortune that the two women could live in the sea captain's house who had owned the property. He had sent a letter stating that he would live out his days in Tahiti and not come back to cold, wet England, thus abandoning the property. Before he left, Hawkins made sure that the ownership papers were correct so the two Jamaicans were not only weavers with a steady form of income but were property owners as well. That put Dominique and Angeline in a unique position among the Jamaicans that populated Portsmouth and Gosport, its sister city across the bay where the women, the hospital, and the sea captain's house and weaving shed were located.

This morning, the two women spent a little time setting up the loom with cotton thread, and then went to their respective places. It took both of them to run the operation and they couldn't fall behind schedule. The demands, both physical and mental, were not inconsequential.

By contract they owed Eli Williams eighteen, three-yard length sheets every week. The sheets were used up in the daily care of the wounded sailors who vomited, urinated, and defecated on the sheets. The nursing staff tried to wash the cotton sheets and some of the old linen ones, but they fell apart under the stress. So, the demand was ever present. Supplying new sheets was a good and steady business, but it wasn't easy, nor was it fast.

The Admiralty forced Williams to pay only two shillings a yard for the cotton sheets. Before he had left for Bristol, Jim Hawkins had arranged for their cotton broker, Jacob Harlow, to buy the cotton and arrange for its preparation for Dominique and Angeline.

The deal they had with Harlow was crucial, for the profit margin they had was slim. Jacob bought the cotton at ten pence per pound, paid towns people two pence a pound for the rough work preparing the cotton, which included scrutching, rough carding, and slubbing. He then arranged and paid for the delivery of the material across the bay to Gosport. In total, Dominique and Angeline had to pay 14 pence per pound for the cotton they had to spin, weave, and sew into sheets.

Angeline was chosen by Jim Hawkins to keep track of all the accounts for the small cottage industry. He had seen the will-to-succeed in her eyes and attitude. Although Dominique was an expert spinner and weaver, Angeline had the education, courtesy of Abigail Stewart, to correctly keep track of the accounting. The young eighteen-year-old seemed happy to accept the challenge and even embrace the responsibility of making sure the two of them were successful.

The schedule they had to meet was demanding. There would be no vacations for these two. Neither could afford to be sick. Spinning never ceased. Actual weaving rarely let up six days a week. Sometimes they agreed to work a half day on Sunday. They could force out anywhere from four to six yards of cloth per day. Then at the end of each day, Angeline would cut and sew the cloth into the sheets of the required length.

In the year that they had been working the business, they managed to net four shillings a sheet after expenses. They had worked over 300 days the first year and had been able to pay Jim and Livian Hawkins back for the loan on the loom. This year, the second year, was when Angeline expected to save close to £60, an almost unheard of amount; a princely sum for a poor Jamaican only recently released from slavery.

Both mother and daughter needed each other, and there was an implicit understanding of that mutual dependency. But there was always an undercurrent of tension between the two. A tension that grew from Angeline's youth and her need for control of her life.

CHAPTER 3

CHAPTER 3

HAWKE STREET PUB
PORTSMOUTH, ENGLAND

John Cady, the mayor of Portsmouth, sat in a corner table of the Hawke Street Pub awaiting the arrival of his chief ally on the city council, one Phil Varlo. The two of them met outside the hallowed city hall and away from prying eyes every couple of weeks, or as situations dictated.

Cady had maintained his mayoral seat largely because the business interests in Portsmouth backed him. He had done whatever he could to make their life easier and for them to make money during the heyday of the slave trade with Africa. Gun and ammunition manufacturers and others who made cloth, brass, tin, and pewter objects wanted safe passage of their material out of Portsmouth harbor. Cady did everything he could to facilitate commerce.

Importers also depended on the docks and the warehousing to run smoothly with cheap labor. They were importing casks of apples, salted beef, deerskins, and skins of other animals from the colonies including fox fur, beaver skins, raccoons, and minks. Because of the rich bounty in the colonies, importers found many customers in England for these commodities as well as American pine boards, salted pork, and of course, huge amounts of sugar, tobacco, and cotton.

Cady often employed extra police when necessary to keep order on the docks. He had the police power under his command and could make life easy for some and very difficult for others. His flaw, however, kept secret by him and a few confidants, was that he was not immune to graft. The shipbuilders and importers knew how to get their goods off loaded and into warehouses without difficulty. All they had to do was get a message to Cady along with a contribution to his re-election fund.

Shippers of slaves into England were also high on the list of protected companies.

Many ships had left Portsmouth sailing to and from the American colonies. Portsmouth rivaled Bristol and Liverpool for the largest number of vessels, but it didn't matter to Cady what place his city had in that triumvirate. Her Majesty's Navy had a commanding presence in Portsmouth. So along with the shipbuilders, Portsmouth was a thriving town as long as there was cheap labor to do the heavy lifting onto and off of ships.

When Varlo entered the Hawke Street Pub, it took a while for his eyes to adjust to the dim light and spot Cady in the corner.

"Where are you Cady, I can barely see you," said Varlo in the general direction of the corner.

"Over here, Phil, over here" whispered Cady. "Don't make a spectacle of yourself."

Varlo slid into the oaken and walnut booth weathered by the backsides of a thousand patrons over the years. "Have anything for me?"

"You get right to the point, don't you Varlo," whispered Cady. "No hello, how are ya, how's the missus?"

"There aren't many people in here," responded Varlo, glancing around the tavern, looking for anyone who might recognize him. "I don't want to be here when the place has a crowd and neither do you, Mister Mayor."

"Right, and there it is, my friend. It's what you came for to be sure." Cady reached into his coat, pulled out a small packet filled with pound notes, and stealthily placed it under the table so Varlo could reach it.

"Don't count it here, you idiot," said Cady. "It's what we agreed on."

"Good. I like it when you reward your allies, John. Makes a lot of sense for both of us," muttered Varlo, sticking the money into his pocket. "Where did you get this, or shouldn't I ask?"

"Can't get through this life alone, I always say. Need the help of friends, strangers, and the occasional enemy."

"Couldn't have said it better. But you were always the man of words, John. That's how you got elected."

"Let's get down to business. There's an entirely new situation that we need to confront head on."

"I'm listening," gruffed Varlo, inching his way a bit closer to Cady to help muffle the conversation that might reach anyone else in the pub. When Cady said he had a situation, it usually meant that bribes needed to be paid, or people needed to be convinced—pleasantly or otherwise—to take another course of action. Varlo had a few men in his district of Portsmouth who would take on jobs when people needed convincing.

"I had a visit from the Naval Administrators, the shipbuilders' association and, if you could believe it, the big cotton importers."

"Bringing in cotton bales from the colonies."

"The same group. They've been bringing in tons of cotton and expect to bring in more and more as the summer wears on, this year and in years to follow."

"What's the problem?" Varlo asked. "They're all getting rich off the slaves in the colonies picking and baling for them. It's not like having to bring the cotton all the way from India."

"No, it's not. But as the shipbuilders put it to me, 'Times have changed and we're not ready to change.'"

"What are you getting at?" asked Varlo, sipping a beer the barkeep had brought him.

"There's been rumored talk of the Jamaicans on the docks and shipyards wanting more money and willing to form a union to get it. I don't need to tell you that if that happens, and they strike, it would mean a shutdown on the docks and shipyards," explained Cady. "The merchants would be furious."

"I see their point. They had slave labor before, and now they have to pay them. How much do they get paid now?" Varlo knew the amount would be smaller than what the white English workers got paid.

"Jamaicans get one shilling a day. Pays for their beer and bread," sneered Cady.

Varlo had heard Cady say that the slaves who worked in Portsmouth were nothing but savages, and Cady openly expressed it, in and out of council meetings. Everyone in the town knew what he thought. His re-elections proved that nobody cared about his disdain for the blacks.

"And the white workers? Never mind, I know. They get two to four shillings a day depending on the skill level. What's the point?" asked Varlo.

"The point, Phil, is that since they've been freed by the Mansfield decision a month ago, they're no longer slaves. Mansfield said it: 'They are breathing free English air just like you and me' and they want more. Simple as that. Since that decision in late June, they've settled for a shilling a day. But they won't continue to do so. That's what the Admiralty and the shipbuilders and the merchants fear."

"How can you stop a union from forming?"

Cady frowned. "I don't know. But I do know that we won't be able to stop it if it gathers a lot of momentum. We could nip it in the bud, so to speak. I'm thinking you and your men could help."

"What do you mean?" answered a skeptical Varlo. He knew what Cady was aiming at but wanted to hear him say it.

"Find out who the union organizer is and pay him a visit. There are always one or two troublemakers, right?" said Cady. "Won't be too hard for you and your men."

"You have a name?"

"The only name that the ship builders heard was a man called Noah."

"Noah? As in the bible Noah?"

"That's what they said. You gonna help with this matter? There are a whole bunch of pound notes in your pocket. Don't ask for more."

"I can pay mister Noah a visit. Maybe dissuade him from his union talk. What about the docks? Got a name down there?" asked Varlo.

"Nobody that's been identified talking union. That's why I have another idea for that group, but I need your help."

"What kind of help?"

"You know the name Sobadu, don't you?" asked Cady. "The so-called magic man."

"Yeah, yeah. What about him."

"I want him to hold those Jamaicans in line down at the docks. Keep their wages right where they are. That's what we're being asked to do. The importers need the labor, but they don't want to pay any more and they don't want riots or strikes!"

Varlo thought for a minute, took a long drink of his flat wheat beer. "Sobadu has a nasty reputation. How will you get him to help you?"

"A little bit of the carrot and a threat of the stick that he will understand. What I need you to do is to get him here. I'll give you a week to make sure he shows up here. Nobody else. What we have to talk about won't be for anyone else's ears."

"I shouldn't need a week," said Varlo.

"Yeah, you might. He's a sly devil."

"How do I find him?"

"He moves around a lot, that's the problem. He'll be somewhere in Buckland with the rest of the blacks. He really doesn't have a permanent address. You can't just go and knock on his door. I hear he's secretive that way. One night he might be with a soldier of his, another night with a mistress. I've only made contact in the past through an apothecary he trades with, a man named Quigley. You can find his shop and pass the message along, agree to have him meet you at Quigley's and then bring him here."

"Listen, Cady, why don't you do this? What do you need me for?"

"Phil, I am the mayor. I can't be caught walking the streets looking for Sobadu. Too many self-righteous folks walking around want to kick me out of office, yet they have no idea what the job really means, and I don't intend on them finding out."

"When do you want Sobadu here?"

"I'll speak to the landlord and we can get a quiet back room a week from now. Can you get it done?"

"All right. I'll go see Quigley tomorrow and we'll get mister big chief magic man here one week from now."

◆◆◆

Ezra Quigley operated an apothecary shop in old Portsmouth. He had learned all of what he knew from his father and uncle who had run the place before they died. That education was in all sorts of both potentially correct and potentially very wrong treatments. In general, he was schooled by his father that people took their own chances in life. He never wanted to intentionally hurt someone who experimented with one of their exotic herbs, potions, tinctures, or oils, but nonetheless never felt accountable if someone died from using one of the so-called remedies he sold.

He didn't follow his father's ancient practice of bloodletting, an old practice where bleeding a patient to remove "bad blood" had been done for 100 years. Bleeding meant cutting into the arm or leg and draining out blood. It was a middle-age practice of quacks. Of course, it weakened the patient rather than remove the so-called "bad-blood."

The people who left their rural roots and came into Portsmouth for work still brought folklore with them that justified myths and superstitions. Ideas handed down from one generation to another had a powerful residual effect, especially since most people in rural England had only a primitive, elementary education if any at all.

Apothecaries often played on these superstitions and sold a bit of hope and expectation with each organic oil or tincture they sold.

Apothecaries also sold purgatives that would lead people to excrete, urinate, or sweat out "bad humors" inside of them. Tinctures of mercury, which in actuality was a poison, were often sold. They were supposed to sweat a disease out, but actually destroyed the stomach lining, caused extreme stomach discomfort, and even death."

Quigley could often forage for his own chamomile, cloves, foxglove, fennel, and white willow bark, but he was reliant on LongAcre Supply in London for some of the rarer, more expensive commodities like myrrh, quinine, marigold and marjoram, and a host of others including poisons and their antidotes.

What Quigley couldn't have sent to him, he bought fresh from people like Sobadu who scoured the local marshes collecting flowers, herbs, roots, toads, snakes, and whatever they agreed might be sold to an unsuspecting customer.

Sobadu and Quigley met in the apothecary shop, but Quigley never knew when he was coming. Slash, Sobadu's right-hand man, would suddenly show up, pull the shades tight so none on the street could see in, lock the door from the inside, and place a closed sign on the door. Once satisfied that no one was in the shop or could enter, Sobadu would enter through the rear door of the shop with a bag containing what he had to trade for. No other customer, nor prying eyes, were allowed in the store when these two men were trading.

On this particular evening, when Sobadu was in his store, Quigley told Sobadu that Varlo had come to see him.

"They want you to meet with them next week at the Hawke Street Pub... back room... ten o'clock at night. Said it was worth your while to show up. Listen to what they had to say."

Sobadu looked carefully into Quigley's eyes for some sign of betrayal, some sign of a trap. He had dealt with Varlo and Cady before and could not afford to trust them.

Sobadu took three steps closer and put his face right up against Quigley's. It was if the reduction in personal space could reduce

Quigley's attempt at any lie that Sobadu could detect. He often did this to people just to intimidate them. It worked on Quigley.

"What do they want? Did they say?" asked Sobadu. He trusted no one, especially a weakling like Quigley who had become a de facto go-between for the white people in power and would sell out to the highest bidder. If Sobadu took him into his confidence, he knew Quigley would share secrets. Because of this, Sobadu told him nothing. Because of this, he never told Quigley anything he didn't expect to get back to Cady, Varlo, or any other white man Quigley might drink with at his favorite pub.

Sobadu had power, but only in the black section of town. He could command the obedience of two hundred men and could form a small army if he wanted. But he had what he wanted at the present and did not want to give it up. If the white boys, mayor, and aldermen wanted to talk to him, they wanted something. Best to find out what it was.

◆ ◆ ◆

Noah had worked in the shipyards for five years. He had worked as a slave, now he was a freeman because of the Mansfield decision. To many of the blacks who were free because they "breathed English air like any other man" their freedom came as a surprise. It took days, weeks, and for some, months to get the idea that they could make their own decisions in life and choose a path that suited them and not their masters.

Noah recognized his right to work as a freeman early, and when the decision came down, he had gone to his supervisor in the shipyards and demanded wages for his work and others starting immediately. That demand from Noah and others like him forced the shipbuilders to pay. They didn't want to pay for labor they previously had for free, save for the penny bread and beer they provided for lunch breaks.

The maintenance work in the dry docks of Portsmouth harbor was hard labor. Not only did the blacks have to scrape visible barnacles off the hulls, but some had to dive under a thin scum of sea water to scrape off barnacles that were partially submerged. Of course, there were no breathing aids to help them, so a man had to hold his breath, dive, locate the offensive sea-bearing shellfish that had attached itself to the ship's bottom, and cut it off. Since there were thousands of these barnacles, the scraping duty could go on for weeks.

Blacks were generally employed in unskilled jobs for the shipbuilders. It was rough, manual work to haul the oak and walnut timbers that would make up keels, ribs, support beams, and planks. Shipwrights and carpenters, one hundred percent white, decided where the wood went and shaped it to the ship's design. Drubbers used adzes to refine the shape of the beams and chipped off unneeded material. But, blacks were the ones who picked up the shavings and hauled them away.

Putting the masts of a sailing ship in place required fifty men. Pulleys helped, but raw muscle power was the key. This was dangerous work, and many times there would be a slip or fall that ended in serious injury. Shipbuilders cared about the safety of their skilled carpenters and shipwrights, but little for the slaves. Now that the slaves were free, they were in a position to withhold their labor if dangerous conditions weren't improved and Noah knew it.

When Varlo's two thugs came calling, it was the middle of the night and Noah had been asleep for two hours. They didn't knock, but burst into the small room that Noah shared with another worker. One thug made a quick move when the other man sleeping in the room woke up first and delivered a quick thump on his head with a small billy-club. The man collapsed in a heap.

The second of the intruders went straight to Noah's bed and yanked him from it. It didn't matter that Noah was clothed in only underwear, having stripped himself of most clothing to sleep in the warm summer air that came gently off the Solent into the boarding house window.

Once out of the straw bed, Noah was slammed up against the wall, facing it. His attacker had grabbed one of his arms and had him in a strong hammerlock, pressing his hand up Noah's back until Noah thought his shoulder would pop out of its socket. The second attacker stood within inches of Noah's ear to add to the intimidation.

"Do I have your attention, Noah?" the brute asked gruffly in a gravelly voice that was barely a whisper. "Are you sufficiently awake so you can hear what I have to say? Nod your head if you can hear me clearly."

Noah nodded with difficulty since his face was contorted because it was pushed against the wall.

"Good. Now listen and listen well. We're here to send you a message. You will *not*. Repeat, *not* speak of organizing a union among your fellow blacks at the shipyards. Some very bad things will happen to you if you continue this talk of money and work conditions. Now I don't expect you to change your ways just because of what I say, so my friend here will help convince you."

The second of the attackers pulled out a set of brass knuckles (which someone had nicknamed "English punch"), curled them in his palm, and delivered three quick but heavily damaging blows to Noah's left kidney. With his face scrunched against the wall, Noah could only grunt in pain. His body went limp and the first of the men released him so he could fall on the floor writhing in pain. One of his kidneys was most certainly damaged and at least one rib was cracked. Noah was not going to be working at the shipyard any time soon.

"Have a good day, courtesy of your city council," one of them sneered as they made their way to the door.

With their message sent, the two street enforcers made a quick exit and vanished into the dark Portsmouth streets.

CHAPTER 4

C ady and Varlo had come separately to the pub to avoid prying and suspicious eyes. Cady had made it his business as a politician to be well known, especially to the admiralty, shipbuilders, and all the commercial powers-to-be. But this was a meeting that he didn't want publicized. Not by anyone.

When Varlo got to the back room of the Hawke Street Pub, Cady gave Varlo some background on Sobadu, the man they were to meet in an hour's time.

"A few years ago I had a drink, well more than one drink as it turned out, with the ship captain who piloted the slave ship that brought this Sobadu character to Portsmouth ten years ago," Cady started, then took a long draught of his flat bitter beer. "As it turns out, he has always been a conniving son of a gun, this Sobadu. He saved his own skin on the slave ship by making a deal with the captain."

"What kind of deal?" asked Varlo.

"The ship came from Santa Maria on the north side of Jamaica and was a slave port of some size. Sobadu was sold with the others. A group of them I understand, as the captain told the story," continued Cady.

"So he was a slave, along with the rest," added Varlo. "I had the impression he was a freeman."

"No, no, he was a slave, but he had some kind of special knowledge of Jamaican herbs—some were hallucinogens, some were tranquilizers. He convinced the captain that he had this special power because of them."

"So why did the captain listen to him? He was a slave. Throw him in the hold with the others."

"You have to look at this from the captain's point of view, Varlo, don't be so thick-headed," said Cady continuing the story. "A captain needs his human cargo to weather a minimum ten-week voyage back to England. And he wants them to be alive when he gets here. What better way than to have the slaves tranquilized."

"Oh, I see. So Sobadu drugs his fellow slaves?" asked Varlo.

Cady nodded. "You got it now. Sobadu convinces the slave master that he would be useful to keep the slaves on board sedated and healthy. Sobadu claimed that he was able to get to Santa Maria with a small supply of what he needed to accomplish the goal for the captain. He even cozened the captain out of some money to stock up on the various herbs before they left port. He tranquilized many of the slaves every day with jimsonweed, Jamaican dogwood, and a whole bunch of other stuff I forgot."

"Pretty neat deal for Sobadu," said Varlo. "He walks the ship freely, escapes the chains, and gets to check on the cargo every day if he wants.

"More than that," Cady continued. "It worked. His 'herbal doctoring' helped calm the overanxious and shackled slaves, not only against the ever-present threat of dying at sea in a storm, but also against the lash. Sobadu told them that when they got to England, he would help them as best he could with traditional Jamaican medicine and help calm them against the tyranny of their slave masters."

"Did they believe him?" asked Varlo.

"Of course they did. The sea captain told other captains and ship owners what had occurred. Sobadu filled a need and was able to keep the Jamaican slaves under his power. On shore, Sobadu's power grew and the slave master continued what he'd been doing. So, de facto he was a freeman, even though technically he was a slave owned by someone. The Jamaicans came to him, obeyed him, believed in him, and so gradually over these past ten years he was given a sort of freedom no other slave had. He had a separate shack to live in and 'minister' to the men after working hours at night. He had total freedom of movement and could go herb hunting during the day down in the Baffins Pond area and in the Farlington Marshes."

"Sweet deal," offered Varlo.

"I'm sure it's all nonsense, but a lot of the blacks believe he has magic powers, that he can heal the sick. I even heard rumors of him raising the dead. Just rumors I'm sure."

◆ ◆ ◆

It was nearly ten in the evening when Quigley brought Sobadu to meet with Cady and Varlo. There were just a couple of details that had to be ironed out before any talking could start. Sobadu stood at the outside doorway with Quigley and Slash. Quigley had not anticipated that Slash would be with Sobadu, but the Obeah man had insisted.

Cady had two members of the constabulary at the door blocking entry for anybody except the invited guests. Cady may not have wanted to have armed guards, but he didn't trust Sobadu.

Quigley knew that if he was to receive anything for his intermediary assistance, he had to deliver only Sobadu to the two officials who were waiting indoors. Slash was a problem. Everyone in the black slums knew Slash, including Quigley, but he couldn't possibly say no to Sobadu when Slash was included in the back-alley trip to the Hawke Street Pub. It was no secret that he was an armed assassin for Sobadu. Slash's chosen weapon was a long sharp machete which he kept at the ready, along with a backup blade strung in a sheath that slung around his neck out of view. The three of them, however, were not prepared to see the two armed guards with muskets blocking the entrance to the tavern.

Quigley spoke first. "These men need to pass. Those are my orders."

"They may be your orders, but they are not ours. Only one man goes in," said one of the guards. "Orders of the mayor."

"I see. Well, go inside and tell him that Sobadu, Quigley, and Slash are outside and want to come in," said Quigley, trying to remain calm standing next to men who could start a fight any minute.

"No, you go in. You alone. We'll stay here and keep an eye on these two," said one of the guards with some authority, holding his musket at a level that would make it easy to use the gunstock as a club.

"As you wish," responded Quigley. He opened the door that led to a hallway and to the back room where Cady and Varlo were waiting.

"Where's Sobadu?" demanded Cady.

"At the door with Slash, his bodyguard," said Quigley. "Nobody knew there would be two guards at the door."

"Just some insurance, Quigley," said Cady. "Can't be too careful."

"You send Sobadu in here without Slash, or whatever his name is," Cady barked. "And you take off as well. Your work is done. This is for you trouble," he said as he threw a five pound note across the table.

Cady continued, "Take this and get out of here. Leave Sobadu to us and tell the guards to keep Slash right next to them. We won't be long with Sobadu. We just want to give him a message."

"Or two or three messages depending on how he takes the first," said Varlo with a snarly chuckle.

Quigley went back outside and spoke directly to Sobadu. He didn't like delivering bad news, but he didn't want to go back and forth down this hallway all night.

"Slash has to stay here with the guards. They say it will be a short meeting. Just a few minutes," Quigley stammered.

He was met with a cold stare from Sobadu, who thought for a moment and then said to Slash, "Stay here. If I'm not out in fifteen minutes, damn the guards, come and get me."

Slash found a wall that he could lean against and keep an eye on the two guards as Quigley scurried away. Sobadu went in and found the dimly lit room.

When he saw that both Cady and Varlo were sitting there, he spoke before they had a chance to. "Make it quick. You have fifteen minutes, then I am leaving."

"No need for even that amount of time, Sobadu," said Cady with a false grin on his face. He disliked most blacks and felt sullied to have to deal with one directly, even to bargain with him. "Go on, sit down. I'll get straight to the point."

Sobadu sat down but not in the chair they had positioned for him with his back to the wall, hemmed in by the table in front of him and the two chairs the mayor and alderman sat in. He quickly repositioned his chair so he would have easy access to the door. He knew they could easily do him harm here in this tavern and escape any sort of white man's justice. To further ease his trepidation, he drew a large knife from his waist and laid it in his lap, making a show of it so that Cady and Varlo could see he was armed.

The two of them had flintlock pistols under their coats but left them hidden. *No need to escalate tension*, Cady thought when he saw the knife. "No need to fear us, Sobadu. No need at all," said Cady. "We've asked you here to conduct business with you."

Now was the tough part for Cady. He had to butter up this black man, praise him for his political strength before asking him to do his bidding.

"You have a lot of power in Buckland, Sobadu. We recognize the hold you have on many of the dockworkers, warehouse laborers, rope makers, and the cotton haulers," gushed Cady practically choking when he gave this accolade.

Varlo finally spoke, "Yeah, Sobadu. You seem to get them to do whatever you want. You've been living well because of it. We don't know how you do it. But it seems to work."

Sobadu kept quiet. He recognized false praise when he heard it. He knew the white men would never relinquish power. He knew that if they could have slaves again, they would do so in a second. The

Mansfield decision was a thorn in their side that they had to deal with, painful though it was. Sobadu could recognize their slimy, patronizing attitude.

Cady joined in. "Well, when the Mansfield decision came down and the word was spread, there were no riots in Portsmouth as there were in other English cities. Somehow you convinced them that they would only hurt themselves if they burned and looted. I didn't have to send militia to walk the docks or put down any riot. That peace was your doing and there is a reward for you for keeping the peace."

Cady slid a packet of pound notes across the table. Sobadu looked at the money and put it in his pocket.

When Sobadu took the money, Cady knew immediately that Sobadu could be bought for anything else Cady wanted. That was the carrot he would dangle in front of him.

"There is more that needs to be done, Sobadu. You can help, and there will be something for you if you do."

"Explain," said Sobadu. The tall black man kept his own counsel—as the saying went—when talking with a white leader. He chose to respond with as few words as was necessary.

"Well, we know the dockworkers get paid one shilling per day. A good wage. A wage that will provide bed, board, and beer," said Cady, watching Sobadu very closely to see what his reaction would be.

"Whites get more," said Sobadu tersely.

"We know that," interrupted Varlo.

Cady shot him a quick glance to let Varlo know that he wanted to be the one to carefully explain what he wanted Sobadu to do.

"Our request of you is quite simple really. We want the blacks to continue to accept one shilling a day," promoted Cady. "Simple as that."

"They want more," said Sobadu.

"Of course they do," responded Cady. "Everybody wants more. But you see, if they demand more, many would be fired, laid off, unemployed. The importers, owners of the warehouses, rope manufacturers, spiral oakum makers couldn't afford to keep as many men working, and we—that means me—might be faced with the unemployed getting in all sorts of trouble, rioting even. The city can't tolerate that. We have a reputation as a city that promotes commerce, and peace for hardworking people."

"Up to now, it hasn't been a problem," Varlo said, throwing his opinion into this conversation.

Sobadu pointed a steely glare straight at Varlo. "As long as you had slaves under your thumb, the whip and the club," said Sobadu. "Times have changed. You must change."

"All right you two. Enough," protested Cady. "If your people are rebellious, we all lose. Including you Sobadu. We will pay you to keep the peace and to keep your people from demanding more money or striking."

"Pay me?" asked Sobadu.

"Yes. Pay you. Let me be clear," said Cady. "Get them to accept the going wage, no riots, no strikes, no union. In return we will pay you every year there is peace. And listen to the rest of my offer. The office of the mayor and the constabulary will let you have control over the area of town where you all live. No questions. Buckland is yours, from Lake Road on the south to Kingston Crescent on the north, Kingston Road on the east, Mile End Road on the west. No police presence past normal patrols that they have now. Unless, of course, you personally call them in."

Varlo felt the need to state the obvious. "That gives you almost absolute control over the blacks in that section of Portsmouth. No rules but your rules. No police but you. No jury but you. You deal with assaults, robbery, even murder. We won't get in the way. You can run your pagan rituals without our interference. We ask a lot of you, but you get a lot in return."

"How much?" asked Sobadu.

When Cady heard that, he knew the deal was done. Now it was just a matter of money. He wouldn't be cheap, but he'd start low just to see.

"Fifty pounds for the first year. More to follow in the next year."

"You want me too cheap," said Sobadu. "Your cotton importers, rope makers, importers, warehouse owners will all profit hugely because of this. You can afford more. Get it from them."

"You can promise compliance?' asked Cady.

"I can promise compliance. Those who disobey me face more than a beating. It is not going to be easy. I will have to employ guards, enforcers of my rules, as you say. It would be my own police force. No. Not fifty. You pay me one hundred pounds today. Three hundred pounds for the whole year."

"Too much," said Varlo, out of turn. This was Cady's negotiation and Varlo had this irritating way of interrupting.

"Two hundred and fifty pounds for the year, and that's it, Sobadu," said Cady hoping this amount would seal the deal. "If you don't accept it. I will triple the amount of police presence in your area. I will make sure that you and Slash and anyone else in your harem will be arrested every week."

"On what charge?!" demanded Sobadu.

"We'll make something up. Witchcraft for starters, disturbing the peace. Assault. We will find something every week, I promise you," responded Cady. "You will spend plenty of money on white lawyers to keep you from being tossed in Bridewell prison, where you will rot like a corpse. Two hundred and fifty pounds it is. You can live like a king on that."

"I already live like a king. People return favors so that I get everything I want, and I mean everything. Two hundred and fifty pounds it is. I'll need the one hundred pounds now to employ guards and soldiers. You can pay me the rest later in the month. And what if I can't control my people?"

"Then, I promise you holy terror and the full force of my office and constabulary will rain down on you," snarled Cady. Now that he had Sobadu accepting a bribe, his true feelings could be revealed. "Any union, any rioting, any strikes, will be dealt with harshly. Since the constabulary is under my control, I will have strikers, or rioters or union agitators rounded up and shot in full view of others so we get the message sent, true and full. And we won't be careful when we establish who is at fault. We will just shoot first. You got that?"

"Yes, we understand one another. The money? I won't leave here without it."

Cady reached to the floor, picked up a wooden box, and pulled out 100 pound notes and gave them to Sobadu. Since most of Sobadu's business up to this point—selling herbs, incantations, and prayers to Obeah had been on a barter basis—this was the most actual money he had seen in the ten years he had been in Portsmouth.

After he took the money, Sobadu rose from his chair.

"One more thing," said Cady. "Next year we will talk again. Until then, do not contact us. Do not come near us. Stay in your own area of Buckland. If I need to talk to you, I'll get Quigley to get a message to you. Other than that, you are on your own."

Sobadu left the room and collected Slash at the door where he and the guards had been holding a staring contest while Sobadu had been indoors. The two black men didn't say a word as they walked swiftly down the back alleys of Portsmouth, back to Sobadu's rooms.

CHAPTER 5

WEAVING SHED
GOSPORT, ENGLAND

Every week, the same demanding schedule drove Dominique and Angeline to work ten hours a day, six days a week. Hour after hour, day after day, they had kept up the pace. The business they had from Eli Williams, the Haslar Hospital administrator, was constant. He would take their weekly production without fail. But it was a double-edged sword. His staff needed the sheets every week and would replace them as their supplier if they had to.

There was another linen and cotton sheet supplier by the name of Henry Pennington who wanted the women's business with Eli Williams. Pennington had pleaded with Williams to give his firm the sheet supply contract, but Eli stood his ground and honored what he had agreed to when Jim Hawkins had been there. The fact that the Jamaican women had taken over Hawkins' operation was of little consequence to him. As long as the sheets arrived every Friday, he wasn't going to change anything. Pennington wanted to charge more anyway and was dissatisfied with the price that Williams paid the women. But the Admiralty had their cost-cutting demands and this was one of them.

The two Jamaican women had accomplished a lot, mostly

because of their will to succeed. Dominique was no less demanding of herself than she was of Angeline, but Angeline had the education and mental acuity to calculate what they needed to do, handle the payments, and expenses.

On Friday afternoon in early July, Angeline was getting the eighteen sheets prepared to deliver to the hospital. She didn't have to give them directly to Eli, she could give them to one of the orderlies. Angeline insisted on someone's signature on a receipt of delivery detailing the number of sheets delivered and at what time and on what date. Jim Hawkins had taught Angeline how to keep records to avoid any misunderstandings, and Angeline paid careful attention these details. Williams was in favor of the detailed record keeping and instructed his often-lazy orderlies to sign the document without giving Angeline or her mother any grief.

With a signed receipt of delivery in her hand, Angeline would go to the administrator's office. Eli or his secretary, Mrs. Hewitt, would file the receipt and pay Angeline out of petty cash. At six shillings per sheet, the eighteen sheets earned the two women close to six pounds a week. It was a godsend that Eli was willing to pay out of petty cash for some of it since going through the Admiralty's payment accounts might take a week to have the deposit credited to the account they had at the Admiralty. Angeline needed cash payment for a good reason. The cotton brokers didn't extend them any credit.

It could have been racial bias on their part or just Angeline's young age, but business credit for this particular cottage industry was rare. Angeline often took only half the money in cash, asking Mrs. Hewitt or Eli to pay the rest into their account at the Admiralty. Jim Hawkins had cautioned her against having excess cash in their house, and she saw the wisdom of that caution.

On this particular Friday, Angeline packed up the sheets and walked the half-mile to the hospital as she had done many times over the past year. She did that with a sense of satisfaction. The air and breeze off the water refreshed her spirit. The salt laden wind gave her a feeling of real peace. Sometimes at night after dinner, she would walk alone to the pier on the east side of the hospital and catch the full wind off the Solent. It was a simple pastime at the end of a strenuous day, but it was invigorating.

The sheets in her large pack weighed about twenty pounds but she didn't mind the weight of them, especially since she only had to carry them a half mile.

When Angeline got near the hospital entrance, she chatted briefly with the guards before going in. She and the guards shared a sense of humor. Angeline's smile was infectious and the guards who had been there over the last six months enjoyed chatting with her. The guards were young men just a year or two older than Angeline, and they flirted with her not only because she made them laugh at a petty joke but because guard work was so inherently boring.

The guards were protective of the two Jamaican women. Early that Spring a couple of them showed Angeline hand-to-hand fighting. They told her that if she ever had to protect herself from being attacked, that she should go for the most vulnerable parts of a man's body, kick his groin, gouge his eyes, jam the palm of a hand into his nose, and stab your thumb into his throat. Kicking a man in the stomach, or chest or anywhere on his upper body, wouldn't do much good in disarming someone who meant her harm.

They showed her how to escape the first onrush of an attacker, maneuver out of the way, and position herself to strike back as hard as she could. With a little practice, though pantomimed, Angeline felt that the young soldiers had given her a valuable lesson. Angeline knew she had strong hands. Working the loom day after day gave her the hand strength of two good soldiers.

On one of her subsequent trips, one of the soldiers first warned Angeline that he would feign an attack for her so she could show him what she had learned the previous week. When he did, she moved, kicked, and punched just as she was taught. She didn't know how to pull a punch or kick, so she came very close to breaking the poor guy's nose.

Angeline was never in a hurry on these Friday afternoons. It was the culmination of a long week. The walk to Haslar, delivery of the sheets, and the walk home might take the good part of two hours. Since Angeline and Dominique had spent so much time together during the week, this brief time apart was good for both of them.

As Angeline was walking to the hospital, Willie Ferris, a carriage driver, stopped his rig next to her on the road. "Want a lift, Angeline?" asked Willie who had grown fond of the two Jamaican women who worked hard at making a world for themselves with their newfound freedom.

"No thanks, Willie, the weather is balmy and I need to stretch my legs a bit. But thanks. Who are you picking up today?"

"One of the doctors wants a lift to the ferry, but I may have to wait awhile. He wasn't sure he would be able to get away for the weekend."

◆ ◆ ◆

Javel was a poor Jamaican, but a tough man who had taken his share of beatings when he was a slave. Standing at roughly six-feet tall and weighing twelve stone, he was a roughneck who made his living doing odd jobs around the dock. On this Friday, he was paid by Jacob Harlow, the cotton broker, to deliver prepared cotton to the two Jamaican women. Harlow didn't have to pay much for the delivery service. Javel was a day laborer who could make a few pence to take the scrutched and slubbed cotton bales in Harlow's wagon, rent a small flatboat ferry to haul him across the bay, and pull a rented wagon cart with the cotton to Angeline and Dominique's weaving shed.

Javel had been to the weaving shed only once previously, but it had been on a Wednesday when both women were working, and the delivery went without incident. In fact, the women didn't even speak to Javel which made him feel awkward and less than human.

When Javel came to the carriage house this Friday, he was not originally filled with evil intent, but he wanted some show of recognition for the service he was providing. He wasn't a slave to these women; he had pride.

Javel noticed that only Dominique was there as he unloaded the bales of prepared cotton fiber. Without a word, Dominique pointed to the place in the shed where she wanted the fiber. It rankled Javel that she didn't speak to him, a fellow Jamaican

"No one here but you today?" Javel spoke first, trying to make conversation as he grunted and groaned putting the bales of cotton in the shed. He was an uneducated man of the Portsmouth docks, so it may have sounded differently to Dominique than what he had innocently meant.

"Yes, that's right," answered Dominique, unwary of being alone with the big man whom she had seen before. "Angeline is at the hospital delivering sheets. What's your name?" asked Dominique.

Her tone of voice was interpreted by the crude dock laborer as condescending and dismissive. "Javel," he roughly answered.

When the bales were unloaded, Javel brought the invoice over to Dominique who was standing next to the carding table. She quickly took the invoice, made her mark with a large capital "D" and thrust the piece of paper back at him.

It might have been her dismissive attitude toward him that set him off, or it was just animal lust. The reason didn't matter when he grabbed Dominique and put his face forward to hers and tried to kiss her.

Dominique put her hands on his chest and tried to push him away. She averted her face to the left to avoid his slovenly attempt to put his lips to hers.

Rejected, he held her tight to him, wrapping his hands around her upper arms and tried again. She was able to get one hand free and slapped him across the face as hard as she could. It didn't faze him, it only made him angrier and more determined.

As a man who fought on the docks, the slap was nothing, but to his gutter brain, being hit gave him permission to hit back. That physical open palm slap was all the brute needed to set him off.

"Stop!" cried Dominique. "Stop! Get away from me!"

Javel pulled his beefy right hand into a fist and slammed it against her face, opening up a bleeding cut from the soft tissue above the eye almost immediately. With the advantage, he shifted his weight to his left side, and like a prize fighter, threw a left hook into her mouth, slicing open her lower lip. Now bleeding from two places, he advanced on her.

He pushed her onto the floor. She sprang quickly from his reach, jumped up, and leapt away from the loom. She was too quick for Javel, and made it to the other side of the carding table where the tools were.

Javel was temporarily blocked by the table but managed to reach across it and grab Dominique by her arm and pull her across the carding table toward him.

He pinned her down with all his weight and started to pull her dress off. But Dominique was not going to give up and submit. On her back, she looked to her right and saw a carder—a hard, flat piece of wood with sharp spikes used to comb the cotton before it was spun. She grabbed it and raked him as hard as she could across his face, the spikes ripping open huge, bloody gashes.

Javel yelled in pain and his hands instinctively went to his face to stem the blood. In an instant, Dominique rolled off the table. She spotted a scissors and clutched it with the blade pointed out as a weapon, moving towards the door, putting the table between them.

Bleeding profusely from the gashes, Javel was in a blind rage. He stumbled over the table, reached out, and almost got hold of her. She made her way to the door but tripped. Javel caught up to her and pulled his arm back to hit her with an open palm. She saw the slap coming and thrust the scissor's blade directly into his right hand. Dominique ducked to avoid Javel's left hand and ran out the door.

Screaming in pain, Javel roughly pulled the scissor blade from his hand and ran after Dominique. With blood running down the left side of her face, she raced past their residence to the road. Rather than stop and face him, she was going to outrun him the half mile to the hospital, where guards were stationed at the gates.

Halfway there, a two-horse hansom carriage came towards her and the driver stopped and got down from his rear perch to see what the trouble was. It was Willie Ferris and he had Angeline as a passenger, who just for a lark had begged Willie for a ride to see what riding in a carriage felt like. Angeline was in a cheerful mood, only looking out the window when Willie stopped the horse and jumped down to the ground.

Angeline then saw her mother. She was fifty yards away and running towards them. Willie wasted no time and ran towards Dominique. Angeline quickly got out of the carriage and ran after Willie. She ran as fast as she could, and since Willie was up there in years, she caught up to him in twenty yards just as the two of them came upon Dominique with her face bloodied and her dress torn.

Dominique was out of breath but pointed back towards her house. "Javel tried to attack me!" she cried.

"You're safe now, Dominique. Where is he?" asked Willie.

Just then Angeline spotted Javel who appeared one hundred yards away. Despite the distance, Angeline could see the blood on Javel's face. She was torn between going after Javel and tending to her mother's wounds.

When Javel saw that the driver of the hansom and Angeline were with Dominique, he immediately turned tail and ran as fast as he could to the Gosport docks.

Dominique collapsed from exhaustion and from the spent adrenaline that had coursed through her body. Angeline asked Willie to get a water canteen from the carriage, and when he returned, she gave some water to her mother who was cradled in her arms.

"I'm going after him! Can you get your mother home?" asked Willie.

"Yes, of course, but I need to let her recover a bit first." Angeline didn't have anything but the hem of her dress to wipe the blood away from her mother's eye and mouth.

After drinking a little water, and feeling safer, Dominique was able to walk under her own power in a few minutes.

Willie had jumped back into his hansom and raced to the docks, but he was too late. Javel was on the ferry, which was already fifty yards from the shore. Willie took a good look and memorized the face of the black man with a bloody gash across his face. *That will stay with him awhile*, thought Willie. *We can use that to track him down.*

CHAPTER 6

THE NEXT MORNING
GOSPORT, ENGLAND

That night, Angeline nursed her mother's swollen lip and cut above the eye but did not venture across the bay to find Javel. It was a warm summer night, and as usual on these nights, Angeline opened the windows wide so the breeze from the river could soothe their spirits. It was an uncomfortable time. Dominique was still unnerved by the attack. Angeline was angry and thinking about a weapon she could use to hurt the man who had harmed her mother.

All the disagreements the two of them had in the past drifted away and seemed meaningless since the attack. Angeline was maturing and was realizing that the two of them needed each other, relied on each other, depended on each other. There were only a few blacks in Gosport with the remainder of the Jamaicans in Portsmouth. Angeline was convinced that they had to assimilate into the Gosport-Portsmouth English culture, but always felt more comfortable with members of her own racial background because of their shared experience as former slaves.

Angeline absolutely loved the independence they had since Dr. Hawkins had left, but in times like these, the independence Angeline craved so much also made her feel isolated and vulnerable.

Willie Ferris had gone home with the understanding that in the morning he would be on the lookout for Javel. He said he would stop in and see how Dominique was doing and hopefully prevent another attack if Javel should return. It was a real possibility since Dominique could recognize him and knew his name.

When morning came, Willie was at the door on his normal trip to the hospital. He had a doctor with him; one who lived in Portsmouth and took an early ferry to Gosport and then transported the mile or so to the hospital.

"I brought Dr. Foreman here to see you ladies," announced Willie as Angeline let him in the front door. Normally, the two women would be hard at work in the weaving shed on a Saturday, but since Dominique had been badly injured, she needed to rest.

"Let me take a look at the patient," said Foreman, a bright young doctor from Edinburgh who had helped Drs. Hawkins and McLaughlin before they'd left Gosport.

"If you two are here, I am going to the constabulary in Portsmouth to see if they can locate this Javel creep," said Angeline, determined to get some justice for her mother.

"No, don't go!" said Dominique. "He won't be back here. Ever! I know his type. He's a coward who will not show his face around here again!"

"Mother, I am going," voiced Angeline. "We're not working today. The doctor will look after you, and Willie will stop by now and again to check on you, won't you, Willie?"

"All day long and into the night if necessary," responded Willie.

"So you don't need me here and I want Javel to pay for what he did," Angeline said with an anger and resolve in her voice. She thought about her bible teachings. "Proverbs said it best. *When justice is done, it brings joy to the righteous, but terror to evildoers.*"

"You need to be careful, Angeline. You'll need some help once you get to Portsmouth," interrupted Dr. Foreman. "I hate to say it, but I have doubts that the constabulary will believe what they hear from a single black teenager."

"Because I'm black or because I am a young woman?" Angeline's voice boomed against the walls.

"Take your pick. There's no telling what excuse they'll come up with to disregard what you say," Foreman added.

"Who do I get then? I am not letting this rest!"

Dominique added quickly to soothe Angeline's mood, "Jacob Harlow has been good to us. Find him, take him with you to the constabulary. He hired Javel. Maybe he knows where Javel lives."

Angeline got the message. She gathered up some petty cash to pay for the ferry rides and strode out the door with a set jaw and disposition to match.

Victor Jerdan was adjusting his sail for the second ferry run of the morning over to the mainland. Angeline spotted him and gave him a few pence for the ride over. Although Angeline was in a hurry, the winds were calm, so the ride would take just a bit longer than normal to traverse the half mile over to the ferry pier at Portsmouth.

"Do you know a black man named Javel?" Angeline asked, wanting to talk to anyone about this crime to try to get some information wherever it came from.

"Mr. Jerdan, this Javel fellow was on a ferry yesterday delivering cotton to us and jumped onto another ferry like yours for the ride back to Portsmouth late yesterday afternoon."

Jerdan answered slowly as he unmoored the bow and stern lines of his medium size sailing vessel. "No, he didn't bring the cotton over on my boat, must have used another ferry. But I gave him the ride back to Portsmouth. He looked like he'd been in a hell of a fight. Left side of his face was bleeding from some deep wounds. Could have been a woman's fingernails, I reckoned."

"No, it wasn't fingernails. It was a cotton carder with spikes that my mother hit him with when he attacked her," responded Angeline.

"Attacked her, you say? Is she all right?" queried Jerdan as he hoisted the single sail. The boat drifted with the breeze out into the bay.

"Yes. But I mean to find this man. Which direction did he go when you dropped him off at the pier?"

"I was busy with the boat at the time, but I think he went towards the Buckland area."

◆ ◆ ◆

When the boat docked, Angeline made straight for Jacob Harlow's office on Queen Street where he conducted his cotton brokerage business. In these times when tons and tons of cotton were coming across the Atlantic, his business was flourishing, so Angeline thought he would be at work on Saturday morning. Sunday might be a day of rest, but not Saturday.

Angeline had been brought to meet Jacob Harlow when Jim Hawkins transferred the loom business to her and her mother. She'd only had a few dealings with him since that time. She paid her bills through the Admiralty account system, so face-to-face meetings weren't necessary. She loathed having to take time from weaving to ferry across the bay just to deal briefly with payment issues.

As she walked to Harlow's office it occurred to her that she had been remiss in thanking Jacob for the help he had given them. At that moment she felt a bit sheepish that she hadn't thanked him.

She walked slowly, thinking about what she had to do while she looked at every black man on the Portsmouth docks. At any moment she might see Javel but wasn't sure what she would do next. She was no match for him in hand-to-hand combat, but then again maybe she was. The soldiers had given her a few tips. But it was one thing to practice the moves in private or spar with the soldiers. It was another thing all together to get into a death struggle with a dock fighter like Javel. She silently hoped that she wouldn't see him. She needed help to catch him.

At Harlow's office, she paused for a moment after she opened the door to see a half-dozen men standing around gesticulating and talking loudly about the business circumstances they were facing. The room was loud, but in the vocal confusion, she could hear Jacob Harlow's voice and waited for a lull in the talking to call out his name.

"Mr. Harlow, can I have a word?" shouted Angeline.

All six men, including Harlow stopped talking when they heard the female voice, and then at least two of the men were visibly unnerved that the speaker was a black woman.

Harlow, seeming to sense the discomfort of his business associates, spoke quickly. "Angeline, dear Angeline what a pleasant surprise it is to see you. Did you bring your beautiful mother with you?"

"Not on this trip, Mr. Harlow, and she's not so beautiful this morning with a swollen eye and a smashed lip."

"What's that you say, smashed lip? Here, here, come into my office. You can tell me all about this." And then to the men standing gaping at Angeline, Harlow said, "Young Angeline is a weaver with her mother over at Gosport. She is a good customer of mine. Just give me a few moments, gentlemen, while I find out what Angeline wants."

Angeline was glad to leave the room where all the white men were staring at her.

When they were in his office, Angeline told Jacob what had happened the previous day. Angeline was direct with him. She was in no mood for idle chat. "Two questions. Mr. Harlow, did you hire Javel to deliver cotton to us yesterday and do you know where he is?"

"Wait a minute. Slow down, Angeline. I can see that you are angry but... no I didn't hire him. I asked one of my warehouse foremen to find a dockworker to take your cotton to you. Didn't cost but a few pence. Plenty of these rum-soaked dock rats will do the job. He probably just went out on the dock and picked someone who was sober enough to get the cotton across the bay safely. I am sorry about your mother."

"I have to find him. Make him pay for what he did."

"Yes, yes, but you.... you're only... how old now?"

"Old enough, Mr. Harlow. Now look. I appreciate all you've done for Mom and me, but I need to find him."

"Listen, Angeline. You have to go to the constabulary. Let the police do their job."

"Take me there then, if you would. I have already been told they won't listen to a young black woman. Help me convince them that Javel is dangerous."

"That I can do. Let me get my son to come with us. Three people making a complaint to the force is better than two. They know me, of course, but Michael can help us. We'll fetch him at the warehouse. Let me shoo these cotton men out of the office and I'll lock up and go with you."

The two of them walked briskly across George's Street over to the warehouse. Angeline waited at the door while Jacob went in to get Michael. When the two of them returned there were now three of them to press Angeline's case to the police. With this support from white men, the constabulary had to listen.

When they walked into the constabulary, they went straight to the desk sergeant named Pembroke and pleaded their case. They were met with a level of indifference that even Harlow could not fathom.

When they had the desk sergeant's attention, Angeline explained why they were there. Although it was difficult, she tried to be patient when she explained what had happened. Since Gosport was part of Portsmouth's constabulary, it fell under their jurisdiction. Angeline naively thought they would take action and immediately track down Javel, since they had a name and a vivid description of a man whose face had fresh, deep wounds.

"So this man Javel attacked your mother in her own house?" asked the sergeant with a sneer in his voice. He was looking at Angeline as if she was a waif from the streets of Portsmouth and not the responsible business owner that she was. "And what is your name?"

"Angeline."

And your last name?" asked Pembroke as he scribbled in his logbook. "And your last name?" he repeated, irritated with her silence at his first question.

"I don't have one, it's always been just Angeline."

Under his breath, the officer muttered, "Just like an abandoned slave woman from the streets."

"The attack took place in their weaving shed," said Jacob, trying quickly to add some of his influence. He had heard what the desk man had said and didn't care for the slur.

"Did she invite the man into the shed?" said the sergeant. "Any eye witnesses?"

"No one else was there," said Angeline. "But I saw her running from him in the streets. Me and Willie Ferris, the lorry driver, saved her from him. He ran away to the docks."

"I repeat myself," said Pembroke, showing his impatience at Angeline for not answering his direct question. "Did she invite him into the shed? Yes, or no?"

"Well, I suppose she did. He was delivering cotton from Mr. Harlow here," said Angeline, recognizing disbelief in the officer's questioning.

"So, I take it she knew the man and what he was there for?"

"Sure. He was supposed to deliver cotton, not attack her," said Jacob, sensing that the desk sergeant was either dismissing the complaint or suggesting that the attack was invited by Dominique.

"See here, officer," said Jacob. "This is a legitimate complaint by a citizen. A free woman—"

"Yes, yes, I know the blacks are free now since last month. And I suppose that we have to answer to their needs just like that of any Englishman, but she is black, and you say the perpetrator in this case was...?"

"Black, sir. Yes, he was a black man," answered Angeline, confused as to why they were getting stalled by the doubting officer.

"Maybe she encouraged his advances," said the sergeant. "It happens you know. Maybe she wanted him and it got out of hand."

"No, no, no!" shouted Angeline. "He smashed her mouth, ripped her dress, and hit her in her eye!"

"You keep your voice down, young lady. I don't see that. She's not here. I have only your word to go on here. We have limited resources. If I have to tell you again to keep your voice down, I will see that you are escorted out of here or arrested! Now, Mister... what was your name?

"Harlow. I am a tax paying cotton broker and I think your condescending attitude is wrong," butted in Jacob.

"We are limited as to what we can do. This sounds like a garden variety domestic squabble to me," said the officer as he scribbled down the name Harlow. "Harlow... I know the name." Pembroke lifted his head and looked at the young man standing next to Angeline and Jacob.

"What is your name, son," directed the officer.

"I am not your son, and the name is Michael," said Michael Harlow with an edge of defiance in his tone. It was the first time he had spoken but he could sense his dad's frustration with this man.

"You've been before me, haven't you Michael Harlow. Oh, yes, I remember. Last year wasn't it? Street fighting. Disturbing the peace. And there was another such occasion, I believe. I try not to forget a face," laughed the sergeant.

"That was last year. I am a changed man after those nights in your jail."

"Yes, incarceration in the hole could change someone, I suspect. Well, listen, Angeline, Jacob and, yes, Michael. I can see why you came here today but, we can't be chasing down every alleged domestic assault as it were."

"So, there is no justice here!" screamed Angeline. "You're gonna ignore this? How can you?"

The desk sergeant looked weary of this back and forth and tried to get the three of them to leave. "If you want justice for an alleged injury to a slave, excuse me ex-slave, see someone who deals out justice to the black people here in Portsmouth," explained the officer as he closed his logbook.

"Who's that?' asked Jacob, although he knew full well who Pembroke was speaking about.

"Sobadu, the name is," answered the sergeant. "He knows everyone, takes care of many of the needs of you people."

"Who is this Sobadu?" asked Angeline, with an angry scowl on her face. If it wouldn't have meant a night in jail, she might have climbed up the podium where the desk sergeant was and given him a right cross and cut his lip just as her mom had been injured. She was raging mad at the brushoff that this policeman had given her.

"Where is he?" asked Jacob. "Do you know where we can find him?"

"Where is he? I don't know. We've been told to leave him alone," said Pembroke. "He keeps the blacks in line and that's all we care about. Now be on your way."

When the three of them left the constabulary, they were alternately angry, frustrated, and disappointed by Pembroke's treatment of their complaint.

"I am lodging a complaint with the city council. Pembroke's treatment of this case was disgusting," said Jacob Harlow, taking out his pipe, stuffing it with tobacco, and lighting it.

"I have to find this Sobadu," said Angeline. "Where do I start looking?"

"Listen, Angeline, this is not easy. It will take more than a one-day trip from Gosport to Portsmouth. It could take days, even a week. I have heard of him," said Jacob. "Most of the cotton importers I deal with know of him, because they said he controls the dockworkers and ministers to them with herbs and such. They may not have had contact with him, but he is very real. He moves around. He's like a ghost, they say. If you ask around the shipyard, the boat builders, the docks, you'll find out what I mean. People say he only deals through messengers. He's almost invisible. Yet, rumor has it that if you want anything done among the slaves, I mean ex-slaves… the Africans… the Jamaicans, you have to go through him."

"Dad, I'll go with her," said Michael. "I think I know the streets of Portsmouth even better than you."

"I'm not proud to say so, but I think you're right," said Jacob. He knew his son was different now, a couple years older and matured because of his mother's early death. That had changed Michael a great deal. He had shown his father that he had changed, and Jacob was proud of him for doing so.

Michael interjected, "I can take her around, see if we can make contact with Sobadu. If he knows where Javel is, he can tell us. We can try and get justice for Angeline and her mother."

"Sounds risky. You don't know what you are getting yourself into," said Jacob.

"No. But I don't think she'll let it rest," added Michael.

Angeline gave him a fierce nod, showing him how right he was.

"And if she tries to do it herself, she'll get hurt, maybe worse," Michael said to his dad. "Go back to the office and then home to rest. We can do what we can today, and if you don't mind, we can let Angeline sleep in our house overnight and keep searching on Sunday."

"Whatever you do," cautioned Jacob, "do not try and apprehend this Javel fellow. Find out where he can be located and we will try again with the constabulary. We'll get Dominique over here to identify him and then maybe the police will arrest and charge him."

CHAPTER 7

THE STREETS OF PORTSMOUTH

Michael Harlow and Angeline left Jacob Harlow at the constabulary to find Javel on their own. It was a risky move considering that Javel was street wise and street tough.

"Your father said we shouldn't try to grab him and haul him in ourselves, Michael," said Angeline, glad that Michael was with her but also mad about the treatment she had received from the police officer.

"We'll see if we can find him first. My dad always errs on the side of caution. That's why he's a successful businessman," said Michael. "I've had a slightly different experience in the streets of this town. I've learned the hard way that you have to be ready to fight and protect yourself. And I am. Always."

Michael stopped abruptly, motioned with his head to Angeline that she should look towards him. She saw immediately that he had a large knife tucked in a sheath in his waist that became visible when he lifted his coat.

"I don't ever show that I have a weapon. I have it in case of trouble."

They walked slowly away from the constabulary, looking at all the different people on the street. There were a few blacks, but mostly white people on a Saturday going about their business.

"What did your dad mean when he said you knew the streets better than he did?" asked Angeline, trying to get an idea of what kind of help she could expect from Michael. He was about five-foot ten inches tall with a sturdy build. He had the sandy locks and unshaven face of someone who enjoyed the outside air rather than that of a broker's office. He was working as one of his dad's warehouse foremen and had developed a strong back and stronger body from helping the now ex-slaves move cotton bales.

"I ran wild for a couple of years. Made my mom sad and my father mad. It was all because of school. I hated it. Couldn't sit still. Wanted to be outside, so I went. I wouldn't listen to her or my dad when they told me what to do. 'Stay in school, listen to the teachers,' they told me. I would have none of it. Mom and Dad didn't kick me out and force me to live on the streets, but they had reason to, that's for sure. I was arrested a couple of times. That police sergeant back at the station knew me and I knew him. Thank goodness, I've changed. I didn't know until before my mother died what pain I had caused her. She made me promise to be a better man now that I've grown up some. And so far, as a promise to her, I have been."

"Did you go looking for trouble?" asked Angeline, somewhat naively. She had spent most of her time in the Gosport area working, or living at home. She hadn't made many trips to Portsmouth and didn't know what a rough place it could be.

"Yes, and no. When you're fifteen, sixteen and someone gives you a smart remark, or a shove, you might just lose your temper without thinking of the consequences. I'm sure I had a reputation… well, as a hothead. Deserved it. But, live and learn, I guess. How well do you know Portsmouth?"

"Not well at all," said Angeline. "I certainly don't know the streets like you do. Where to find things… where to find people."

The two of them passed the Portsmouth Cathedral also known as St. Thomas of Canterbury Anglican Cathedral.

"Have you seen this church before?" asked Michael.

"Maybe once," replied Angeline. "Dr. Hawkins took me and Livian over here for a short tour."

"Do you see the lighthouse on top of it?"

"Sure. It's on every night. Isn't it a beacon light for the ships?"

"That's right. It's a symbol of Portsmouth's motto. 'Heaven's Light Our Guide.'"

"You and your dad go to this church?"

"My dad goes more than me. Ever since Mom died, he goes more often. I think maybe he gets in touch with her spirit in there. You go to church?"

They walked for a while as Angeline thought long about what her answer might be. "Well, no, not a lot. I was raised in Jamaica by the people who owned my mom and me before we were freed. The Stewarts were Scottish Calvinists. I suppose that's close to being an Anglican, I guess. Mrs. Stewart made me study the Christian bible. Wouldn't let me practice the rituals my mother does."

"Rituals? You mean she's not Christian?"

"No. She believes in the spirit of Myal. The kind, loving, giving, protecting spirit of nature."

"Sounds interesting."

"Well, Mrs. Stewart said it was pagan worship, like Haitian voodoo. She could be quite mean about it, but she let my mother do what she wanted. But I had to follow the Christian teaching. My mother accepted it because we were owned by the Scottish and one of us had to adapt to their ways, including religion. I was given a bible by Mrs. Stewart as a gift when they sold us on the Isle of Wight."

"Does that crystal you wear around your neck have anything to do with this Myal god your mother prays to?" asked Michael.

"In a way." Angeline took the crystal in her right hand and fingered it gently. "I was told it's a piece of quartz. My mama got it for me when we were first on the Isle of Wight. Sometimes it tingles when I touch it. That's supposed to mean it's my lucky stone meant only for me. The woman who sold it said it was a healing stone. My mother sometimes takes it from me and prays to Myal, the goddess, to protect me."

"I learned something on the street that they don't teach in churches or in schools. You make your own way in this world. No god or goddess is going to help you," said Michael.

"Something like, 'God helps those who help themselves,'" recited Angeline from her bible quotes the Stewarts taught her.

"Yeah, something like that," responded Michael. "Look, we're almost to the docks. I don't think we should split up. But we need to find someone who can tell us where this Sobadu character is." Michael readjusted his waist belt to secure his knife in the case of an emergency. "But I have an idea that will help us. If we talk with a white foreman or white dockworker, I'll ask the questions. They may sneer at the idea that a white man is walking the docks with a black girl."

"A black woman," interrupted Angeline, with a touch of resentment in her tone of voice.

"Right. A black woman," accepted Michael with a grin. The difference in their ages might be two years. Michael was just getting used to Angeline's quick temper if she felt slighted. "But you let me do the talking in that case. If we try to get some information from a black man, you talk. We might have better success that way than if we both butt in."

"Good idea," said Angeline. "You don't seem to mind that I'm black and you're white. Is that your religion talking?"

"No. I'm pretty sure it isn't. But I don't think it's the case for most Anglicans. I'm a little different… in a way. A year ago or so, I wandered down the street to where John Wesley and George Whitehead preached. They were rebels according to the Anglicans, but I thought they were right. They made sense, even to someone like me who didn't—and doesn't—like to read or even think about religion. They convinced me that all men are created equal. And that we British have been dead wrong about slavery. So now I listen to what people say and watch what they do, regardless of their nationality or skin color. I have had to work with people from all over the world in a shipping port like Portsmouth. I make my own decisions."

◆ ◆ ◆

Over the next hour, with Angeline at his side, Michael talked with some dock foremen and Angeline spoke to a couple of the laborers. They were getting nowhere until Angeline talked with a dock worker named Vincent.

"Ezra Quigley, the apothecary. Yup. That's who I heard knows Sobadu. You're right to say that he moves around. He tells you if he wants to see you and then it's always at someone else's home. He doesn't want to be found. He finds you."

"Why Quigley?" Angeline asked the black dockworker.

"Oh, I suppose because the two of them trade healing herbs and such. Sobadu does business with him."

Angeline asked with an insistent tone, trying to learn as much as she could, "Why is Sobadu so important to you? How do you know all this?"

Vincent continued, "I've done some errands for Sobadu to pay off a debt or two I owed him. But Sobadu is a medicine man. He helps us. Provides herbal medicine to us. Grants us wishes. Keeps us safe. Got us paid when we was made free. We could have rioted. We didn't. Sobadu told us 'no trouble. Everybody will get paid,' and he saw to it. 'You will be paid for your work,' he said. And we are. One shilling a day. Three months ago we were slaves, now we get one shilling a day."

Just then with a view over their shoulders, Vincent saw someone lurking near a building staring at him. His demeanor changed immediately and he clammed up. "But, God almighty, do not tell him that I said anything. That's enough. You want this man, you go find him." And with that Vincent abruptly turned and practically ran away glancing over his shoulder at the wall behind where Angeline and Michael stood. When Michael turned around, no one was there.

As they resumed their walking, Michael said, "Vincent says its one shilling a day. Well, it should be two shillings at least. That's what the white dockworkers get. That's the going rate. I wonder how that happened."

Angeline shrugged. "Let's just find this Quigley character. If we're lucky, he'll be in his shop," she said, bursting ahead almost running.

"Slow down, I need to show you where his shop is," responded Michael, trying to catch up to Angeline.

◆ ◆ ◆

"I don't know where he is, and that's the God's truth," swore Quigley slyly when the two young people burst into his apothecary shop demanding to know where Sobadu was.

"Besides, even if I knew, why should I tell you?"

Quigley's shop was full of herbs, either hanging from the ceiling or in small vials. There were tinctures, oils, potions and poisons, and even a couple of skulls. The room was dark, and the only light came from the street. And as it was a cloudy day in Portsmouth, there was scant lighting. Quigley seemed to prefer it this way. There wasn't a single lamp or candle lit. It gave the room an eerie feeling. It certainly had the oddest variety of smells. So many different herbs, so many different smells. They all seemed to blend together into a pungent, almost unhealthy smell. *Not a smell you would want to be inhaling every day,* thought Angeline. She wondered what effect it had on Quigley.

"Who are you and what do you want Sobadu for?" questioned Quigley. He was a man small of statue and looked at the world with a wary and suspicious eye. He didn't care much for people. To him the apothecary business was just that, a business handed to him by his father to make money off the weak. He had herbs and oils that actually did some good, but he would also play to peoples' superstitions to make a sale of some quack tincture or tonic. His unsaid motto was that "if people thought something might work, maybe it would."

"I'm Michael Harlow, son of Jacob Harlow the cotton broker," said Michael. "We need to locate Sobadu. Can you tell us how to get in touch with him?"

"Maybe, maybe not," responded Quigley. "He tells you if he wants to see you. It ain't the other way around, if you get my meaning. Now again, before I lose my patience and throw you out of here. What do you want him for?"

Angeline spoke up with a determined and slightly angry voice. She was irritated at the attitude this scraggly, wizened man was showing them. "We need to locate the attacker of my mother. We were told Sobadu will know how to find a man named Javel."

"Maybe he can and maybe he can't. What is it you do, young lady?" asked Quigley.

Ignoring his condescending tone, Angeline said to Quigley, barely controlling her anger, "My mom and I weave cotton sheets. She was attacked by Javel. The police told us to find Sobadu if we wanted justice."

"I see. You want justice. The police don't give a damn about blacks hurting blacks, do they?" Quigley had a small private chuckle. "Justice is hard to get these days on the streets of Portsmouth, eh, Michael Harlow. Your name is coming to me. My brain's slow but some of the memory comes back."

"Just tell us where to find Sobadu and we'll get out of your hair," snapped Michael.

"Not that easy. Even if I were to help you. There is payment to be made, to me and to Sobadu should he help you. You have money?" Quigley paused, and when he saw the shocked look on the two young peoples' faces, he responded. "Just as I thought, you want something but are willing to give nothing in return. Good day to you both. Beat it!"

"I'll weave you sheets," blurted Angeline. "Just for you and for Sobadu."

Quigley's eyebrows shot up. "Oh, well, that would be nice. Very nice. A good offer. But there will be some payment in coin up front, before I lift a foot or finger to find him."

Michael thought for a moment. It was not like him to trust anyone on the streets of Portsmouth, much less this man, but he relented knowing that the two of them were somewhat at the apothecary's mercy. "I'll give the one shilling I have in my pocket and that's all," offered Michael.

"Accepted," said Quigley. He then paused a moment before continuing. "I'll take your offer and your request to him. Sure. I'll do that. Sheets you say. Fresh sheets. That would be just fine. Couple of sets for both of us should do. It may take a few hours to reach him. He is an elusive devil. Always has a platoon of men who protect him from outsiders, night and day. All the blacks fear and respect him, don't you know. I don't know if I can get to him today, is what I'm saying. But I can close up shop for a few hours and try to find him, as my good deed for the day, mind you."

"How will you reach us?" asked Michael.

"You can't stay here. That's for sure," answered Quigley.

"We can go to a pub and get something to eat. You can contact us there," responded Michael.

"Where then?" asked Quigley.

"Say Hawke Street Pub. You know it, don't you," said Michael.

"Yes. Yes, I do."

Quigley escorted them to the door and not so gently pushed them in the back to get them to leave. Neither resisted but they wanted to. Their youth and physical strength would have made it easy to push Quigley to the ground, but they held back, deciding that if they were to see Sobadu, this charlatan was their only hope.

When they were outside the shop and had walked a few yards away from the front window of Quigley's Apothecary, Michael suddenly stopped and abruptly pulled Angeline aside into a small narrow alleyway.

"What are you doing?" demanded Angeline.

"Be quiet for a moment. Here's what we have to do." Michael quickly looked over Angeline's shoulder so he had a view of the apothecary's front door.

"I'm going to follow Quigley," said Michael. "We can't trust him, and if we know where he's going to find Sobadu, we'll know and we won't have to trust him, use him, or pay him again. He seems to be the kind of man who'll squeeze the last drop out of a lemon if he can find one."

"What am I going to do?" asked Angeline.

"Go to the Hawke Street Pub. I'll give you directions. It's not far from here. Maybe a half mile walk through the city streets. Do you have any money?"

"Not much. What I have I was saving for the ferry ride home later."

"Here's some more." Michael reached into his pocket and gave her some pennies. "This will get you and me some lunch. It's all I have left. Get something to eat and drink and I'll join up with you later," said Michael quickly. If Quigley came out and rushed away, Michael didn't want to lose him.

"I should be with you in under an hour. After I find out where Sobadu is holed up, I'll rush to the pub and beat Quigley there. It's almost certain I can run faster than he can."

Michael quickly gave Angeline some directions and pointed her in the right direction. When he was done, he went to the other side of the street to get a good view of the apothecary shop, ready to tail Quigley once he came out.

The two of them parted company and at once Angeline felt both nervous and confident, a strange combination of excitement and fear. She was alone on strange streets in a city she barely knew, but she had a mission. With a sudden rush of determination, she felt the revenge of royal blood she knew flowed through her veins, took a deep breath, thought about the trauma her mother had suffered, and walked quickly to the tavern.

When she entered the Hawke Street Pub, the noise from men at the bar talking loudly jolted her hearing for a moment. The pub smelled like stale beer on a Saturday when many men were either not working or taking a lunch break before finishing off their work day. It was if being slightly inebriated would help them cope with the six-day work week.

Angeline found a corner seat against the wall, and when the barman came, she ordered a beer and lunch food.

"I'll bring the beer, help yourself to the fish stew from the cauldron at the fire and the bread. Payment first, young lady, house rules, payment first," the barman said with a sneer, as if suggesting that the black woman in front of him might be a freeloader.

"How much?" Angeline asked.

"Tuppence, for both food and the beer."

Angeline wanted to assert herself after the sneer she saw on the barkeep's face. She thought it was too much but gave the man the two pence of her own money that she had saved for the ferry ride home. She kept Michael's pence in her pocket intending to either give it back to him or use it to buy him food and ale when he arrived. Which she hoped would be soon.

The barkeep seemed to examine the money she gave him, looking down at her with a look that expressed his doubt that the money was real.

Angeline waited until the beer was delivered to her along with an empty bowl and spoon. She kept a leery eye on the men at the bar who kept glancing in her direction. She got up with her bowl and spoon and went to the open fireplace from which hung a kettle warming the fish stew. She ladled herself some, grabbed some bread that was on a nearby table, and was making her way back to her table when a man roughly elbowed her, causing her to spill some of the stew.

"Hey, blackie, too much stew for you to carry? What you spilling it for?" The man laughed at his crude jeer and was joined in a mocking derision with his pals drinking at the bar.

"You don't belong here. Go with your own people," a voice growled.

"Stay in Buckland, where you belong," another voice shouted.

Another man said something vile as she steadied herself and continued her way through the crowd to her table.

"Did you hear what I said?" continued the second man who had now separated himself from the group and was standing right in front of her. "Go home. Get out of here."

Another voice yelled out, "Slaves don't belong here."

She sidestepped around the man who had tried to block her path, got to the table where her beer was, set her bowl down, and then turned and faced the last man who had yelled at her.

Angeline was going to have to confront these men. The anger she harbored from her mother's attack had been boiling inside her, and it propelled her to defend herself.

"I have just as much right to be in a public house as you," shouted Angeline, not afraid that the entire crowd could hear her voice. "I am a free woman and I can prove it. I didn't need any judge's order to free me. I was given my free papers a full year ago."

"Free or not, get out!"

"No, I will not!" Angeline moved to sit down, but before she settled into her seat, she was grabbed by the collar of her jacket with a strong hand, a hand that was used to grabbing tar-coated ropes on a sailing ship.

The man who grabbed Angeline pulled her from her bench seat. "Then I'll pull you out of here!"

The crowd hooted as the drunk patrons of the pub egged on the drunk to give his boyos a show.

She was in a fight now, and her training from the soldiers came back to her. *The vulnerable spots. Go for the vulnerable spots. There are no rules. The only rule is to put the opponent down so that he stays down. It's not sparring any longer. It's not pantomime.*

Angeline wriggled free enough to loosen up her right arm. She had been pulled to the floor on her knees. While the brute was trying to pull her by her coat, she planted her foot firmly to the floor, found some support and leverage, quickly cocked back her fist, and unleashed a righthanded knuckle punch into the man's groin as hard as she could. She had the muscle strength to make it count. Hours and hours on the loom had toughened her upper body.

The man took his grip off Angeline's collar for a second as both his hands went to his midsection and he buckled to his knees in pain.

"You guttersnipe!" he exhaled with difficulty.

Angeline knew if the man got up, he would be much bigger than she. Her instructor's warning came to her. "Finish it if you can. Don't let him back into the fight."

Angeline rose from her awkward position, stood, took careful aim, and kicked the man hard in the jaw. She instinctively kicked with her left foot. *Strange*, she thought, *I hadn't known that before*.

The kick connected perfectly and the drunk who had attacked her was lying on his side knocked cold, with blood running from his nose onto the roughhewn floorboards of the tavern.

The crowd had taken a step back as all cowards do when they see one of their own beaten, and Angeline's voice rose to the fiercest, biggest roar she could muster. "I said!" she yelled. "I belong here just as much as any of you! I am a free woman from Gosport and I will beat any man who attacks me! Any man. If you want more of this, I'll have the soldiers from Ft. Moncton over here tomorrow to beat all of you into the ground! If you don't back off, you'll feel the butt of their muskets 'till you bleed!"

Angeline stood her ground staring at the crowd of men who couldn't do more than gape at her, trying to process what they had witnessed. One of the group came and pulled the fallen man out the door. Angeline sat down, and with one eye on the crowd, ate her stew and drank her beer until Michael arrived. She was breathing heavy, but the gut feeling she had was exciting. She liked it.

Not one of the yellow belly drunks at the bar said another word to her.

CHAPTER 8

SOBADU

Sobadu sat in a chair in a room that was rented by Delroy, a Jamaican dockworker. Delroy sat close on his straw mattress facing Sobadu. A candle on a small table burned in front of Sobadu. Slightly above the burning wick was a small tripod with a brass plate holding burning jimsonweed which Sobadu and Slash had collected from the Southsea marshes.

Jimsonweed incense was known to produce amnesia, delirium, and suggestibility. It was this "suggestibility" effect which Sobadu was counting on to sway Delroy to do his bidding.

"My wife has left me," said Delroy. "Can you bring her back?"

"No. I cannot bring her back," said Sobadu. "But take a strong breath above the burning incense. It will help calm you."

Delroy took a breath.

"There, now don't you feel better?"

Delroy was starting to feel the effect of the jimsonweed. He felt a bit delirious, but also euphoric. As he took another deep breath with his nostrils just above the small plate, his euphoria increased, and he was more relaxed than ever. Life wasn't so bad. Perhaps he would be better off without a nagging wife.

Sobadu chanted softly, "Obi-loa – Oh… ANA-LEA-MAH."

"Chant with me, Delroy," Sobadu cloyed. "Chant with me. Pray for better days ahead from Obeah." They chanted softly together.

> Obi-loa- Oh…ANA-LEA-MAH
> Obi-loa- Oh…ANA-LEA-MAH
> Obi-loa- Oh…ANA-LEA-MAH

"Obeah brings relief and healing to those who believe. You do believe in Obeah, Delroy, do you not?"

"Yes, yes, Sobadu, I believe."

"Good, take another deep breath of the sweet smoke."

Delroy did as he was asked, and breathed deeply. His eyes closed momentarily as he savored the euphoria, finding peace in the smoke of the brain-altering herb.

Sobadu continued, "Obeah will bring you peace. Do you believe that, Delroy? Come with me, Delroy. Come with me on a journey to a world that gives you peace."

Delroy leaned back against the wall and let the wall hold up his head.

Sobadu spoke softly and helped Delroy think about the power that Obeah had on him. Delroy's stupor became even more pronounced as the drug's effect grew stronger. Sobadu intoned his call for the loa, the spirit god, to bring peace to Delroy.

"By the power of the Ashanti, your tribe from Africa. Oh, my Obeah. Oh, my Obeah, I offer you food and home. I offer you incense. I call on you to be in our presence. Bring help to Delroy, your servant. Bring him peace. Oh, my loa, you are the living thread between life and death. Come bring him peace. Cure him of his heart's wounds. Your powers are great, my Obeah. Help him."

Sobadu lifted his head from glaring at the candle to see that Delroy was asleep in his narcotic dream.

◆ ◆ ◆

A half hour later, Delroy awoke and Sobadu spoke to Delroy, bringing his face within inches of Delroy's. "You feel better now.

These things that hurt you are gone. They are to be forgotten. Your payment to me will be simple. I am going to ask you to do things for me. You will be pleasing Obeah. Your spirit will be lifted. Will you do this for me. Do it for Obeah?"

"Yes, I will. Yes, Sobadu. What is it you want?"

"Nothing now. But in the future—in the future when I need a favor, will you do that for me?"

"Yes, Sobadu," said Delroy in his dream state.

"Good, that's good. You are good, Delroy. You will find happiness. I can see in the smoke of the incense that you will find joy in the future, much overwhelming joy. Your life will be free and great," intoned Sobadu, knowing he was creating another unpaid servant.

There was a knock on the door, and Slash appeared. Sobadu got up from his chair and went to Slash, leaving Delroy to wake slowly from his dream state.

"Quigley is here and wants to talk to you."

"All right, ask one of the other guards to take Delroy and get him some water, put a couple of pence in his pocket, and send him on his way. Bring Quigley up and stay in the room while he is here. We will both want to hear what he has to say. Chances are he's asking for something."

Quigley had found Sobadu through three layers of security. The first man Quigley found was his normal contact. That man knew where the second man was, and the second man knew where the third man was, and the third man knew where to find Slash. Sobadu would always be close to Slash.

It was a layered security system and allowed Sobadu to move from room to room, woman to woman, and only have to tell Slash, a devoted bodyguard where he would be. Slash had only to notify one man. Sobadu's exact location would be known only to Slash. Sobadu had followed this over the past ten years that he had been in Portsmouth. He wanted to be in control of whom he talked to. He wanted to be in control of his privacy. He wanted to be free to move as he wished without interference and without someone like the police following him.

Sobadu used Quigley as he used everyone else. Quigley was his go-between with the white establishment; the white people in power and in control of the police. The city's power structure answered to their council. They in turn answered to the Admiralty and to the shipbuilders and merchants. But Sobadu knew he controlled the blacks, controlled the unskilled labor needed to get the actual work done.

He was the only one who knew that the mayor had paid him to quell any disruptions by the black Jamaican workers on the docks when the Mansfield decision was handed down. The ones who did the grunt work building ships answered to him as well.

He was face to face with Quigley whom Slash had brought up the stairs. "What are you doing here?" demanded Sobadu.

"I had a visit from a white man whose father is a cotton broker and a black Jamaican woman, both young. She's a weaver."

"What did they want that would bring you here on a work day to find me and disrupt my business?" Sobadu said with some irritation. He never wanted Quigley to think that he, Quigley, was anything more than a messenger, albeit to the more powerful white establishment whose favor he needed as a source of revenue. "I suppose they paid you to bring a message to me. You're always willing to sell your services for a few pence, Quigley. It's what makes you so dispensable and disgusting."

Quigley shifted his weight, looking uncomfortable. "They went to the police when the young woman's mother was assaulted and the police told them to ask you for justice."

Sobadu roared with a derisive laugh. "Justice!! Black man's justice for black men and women. The white police are willing to give up their authority to me. They can be so lazy! That's right where I want them. They're frightened to come into this section of town. The weaklings! They've given up trying to arrest me as a black witch serving the pagan needs of ignorant immigrants. They've given up on taming me. They acknowledge my power, Quigley. I have them!"

"Like I said, the young woman's mother was attacked by some man named Javel," stuttered Quigley. When Sobadu went on a near-hysterical rant such as he had, Quigley thought his life was in danger. One nod to Slash, and he would be dead on the floor.

"Javel?" Sobadu asked. He looked over Quigley's shoulder to see if Slash recognized the name. When Slash nodded in the affirmative, Sobadu's attention came back to Quigley.

"All right, let's say we know him. Let's say we can find him. Let's assume that we can hold him. I don't know why it's important for me to do anything. Someone was attacked. Someone escaped justice for the attack. So what? How does that benefit me? Huh, Quigley, how does that benefit me?"

"Well, all I can say is that you have done this in the past when blacks have harmed blacks. That's why the police think you can mete out justice in this case as well."

"I don't have to be told by the likes of you or them what I am able to do," snarled Sobadu, his mood shifting radically due to the jimsonweed smoke he had inhaled with Delroy. It did not make him delirious, it just boosted his maniacal egoism.

"Well, since it is a white man and a black woman asking for your help, helping them would enhance your standing," ventured Quigley nervously. "Word will most certainly get back to the white importers on the docks. It would let them know you have power over the black laborers. Since they've just been freed from slavery, it wouldn't be bad to reinforce your image."

Sobadu thought for a moment. "Sometimes, you are more clever than I take you for, Quigley. Sometimes, you make sense. Do you know where these two are—the white man and black woman?"

"I know where they told me they would be."

"Bring them here. You have one hour and then I am gone. You hear me? One hour. And what did they offer you for your help in finding me?"

Quigley decided to share only part of the payment information. He left out the money Michael had given him. "Sheets. I'm to get cotton sheets from the young woman. So are you."

◆ ◆ ◆

Michael Harlow had hidden himself like the street urchin he once was and tailed Quigley all the way to the rooming house. He had seen Quigley enter and go up a flight of stairs. Michael didn't need much more. He noted the street name and the house number and made his way as fast as he could back to the Hawke Street Pub.

Michael found Angeline sitting in a corner eating and drinking her beer. He didn't think anything of it, a young woman drinking beer. The English beer sold in alehouses was a rough beer with a very short shelf life. People drank it morning, noon, and night as a source of carbohydrates. It was in the newspapers that each Englishman or woman drank upwards of fifty gallons a year.

"I got here as soon as I could. Quigley took his time getting to the right rooming house. I assume that when he went up the stairs to one of them, he found Sobadu. Anything happen while I was gone? Are you all right?"

"Had a scuffle when I first came in. Nobody has bothered me since," said Angeline. She could have gone into a long explanation of the fight she had been in but decided not to.

The barkeep came over and asked Michael what he wanted. "Beer and food?"

"If you would," said Michael.

"Fish stew's on the kettle and I'll bring you a beer. You with this woman?"

"Yes I am. Any problem?"

"No problem, sir. But I'd be careful with this one. She packs quite a punch." With that quip the barkeep walked back to the bar.

"Must have been a bit more than a scuffle," commented Michael.

"I'll tell you about it sometime," answered Angeline, taking a long slow sip of her beer.

"Okay. We'll leave it like that for the time being. I have no idea if Quigley was successful; this might just be a wasted afternoon. There's no telling if Sobadu will actually help us. We have to think of a back-up plan."

The two of them were hashing out different ways they could find Javel other than depending on Sobadu when Quigley came in through the door.

Quigley walked straight to them. "He'll see you, but you have to hurry. He'll be gone in about a half hour and it will take us that long to get back to where he is. Come now or forget about it."

Michael didn't even wait for his beer and was up out of his bench seat and moving towards the door. Since he had tailed Quigley, he knew where they had to go and how long it would take to walk there.

◆◆◆

"So, what is your name, young woman?" asked Sobadu when Angeline and Michael were in Delroy's room facing Sobadu. Sobadu had already dismissed Quigley, who left to go back to his shop.

Slash maintained his viewpoint of the entire room, huddled in a corner, a knife in his hand, ready to defend Sobadu if necessary.

"Angeline is my name."

"And you, Quigley tells me you are the son of a cotton broker."

"Yes. My name is Michael Harlow."

Michael felt uneasy with Slash in the room. If there was going to be trouble, he wanted to be prepared for it. He'd never met Slash before but had heard of his reputation on the streets. He was known to have killed people and never been arrested.

"Tell me what you want with Javel," Sobadu said. All four people were standing in the room; no one was sitting. It was as if all four were facing each other in a duel. The atmosphere was tense. The smell of jimsonweed still was present, though not strong. Slash's presence added an element of danger in addition to the imposing size of Sobadu who was larger and taller than most blacks in the Portsmouth area. He commanded the room and let people know it. He would take deep breaths every so often and puff his chest out and make quick hand gestures toward the two young people, as in a feigned slap.

"Javel attacked my mother at our weaving shed in Gosport," started Angeline. Though a lot younger than Sobadu, her fight earlier in the afternoon had given her a newfound feeling of strength and confidence. "He tried to rape her in the shed. She fought back and got a bad cut on her eye and a badly cut lip in the fight. I want... we want him to pay for what he did."

"And you went to the police?" asked Sobadu, even though he knew the answer. He wanted Angeline and this Michael to acknowledge that he had police power.

"Yes, and they said to come to you, since it was black on black violence," said Michael.

Sobadu cast an eye on Michael and moved suddenly towards him, stopping just inches from his face in an effort to scare him.

"Boo!" said Sobadu loudly.

Michael didn't flinch. His adrenaline level kicked up, but he did not move, standing his ground.

Sobadu just laughed. Then he continued his verbal attack looking menacingly at Michael. "One black man attacks a black woman and the white police won't do anything. Sounds familiar. That's what they think of us, that we are savages and need to police ourselves," said Sobadu.

Then Sobadu quickly turned his attention to Angeline. "Tell me that you need my help... my justice. Tell me," commanded Sobadu. "I want to hear you ask."

"I need your help," said Angeline.

"We need your help," said Michael, reluctantly.

"Good. That's good," said Sobadu. "What do you offer as payment for this service?"

"My mother and I weave cotton sheets for Haslar Hospital. We can make you cotton sheets," offered Angeline.

"Make ten of them," said Sobadu "And I will find Javel for you, even deal out justice if this attack on your mother is true. But that will not be enough. For justice to be done, your mother will have to identify him so we will know we have the right person."

"You will be able to recognize him easily. My mother raked a carding board across his face. He bears the scars."

"No. That's not enough. Your mother will come and face her attacker. Face him. Accuse him to his face in front of us and his fellow Jamaican brothers and sisters and we will see what justice they will decree... if any," dictated Sobadu. "That is my decision. Now leave."

"When and where does my mother have to do this?" asked Angeline.

"Bring her next Sunday afternoon at four to the Kent Street Warehouse. It's near the docks. Bring the sheets. And do not bring this white man or any other white man with you. It would not be safe for him. Not safe at all. Now leave. Tell me, what is your mother's name?"

"My mother's name is Dominique."

The look on Sobadu's face turned. His mouth and lips changed from a huge dominating grin to a frown in a split second. Even Angeline took note of Sobadu's widened and stunned look in his eyes. He almost looked scared to her.

Why would my mother's name do this to him? Angeline thought.

"Did you say Dominique?" asked Sobadu, his voice no longer gruff and demanding, but weak and shaky.

"Yes, I did. What does it matter?"

"Is she Jamaican?" asked Sobadu quickly.

"Of course, as I am. I was born on the island eighteen years ago." Angeline wondered why this witch doctor had so many questions.

"And who is your father?" demanded Sobadu, regaining his composure.

"I was a small child when my father died in Jamaica," said Angeline. "I only knew him by one name. He was called Tacky."

CHAPTER 9

GOSPORT

Even though she was young, after an incredibly long day, Angeline was dead on her feet. She had even nodded off on the short ferry ride from Portsmouth harbor to Gosport. Victor Jerdan, the ferry boat's operator woke Angeline when they landed, and helped her step to the dock so she could walk the half-mile home. As Angeline made her way, she tried to make sense of all the things that happened, from the meeting with Quigley, the fight in the pub, and the almost terrifying meeting with Sobadu. It was a jumble of emotions that she had trouble straightening out. She wanted to take strength from what had occurred, but it was difficult.

When she arrived home, rather than go straight to bed, she needed to see how her mother was doing

"How are you feeling?" asked Angeline when she walked into her mother's room. Angeline could see from the idols on the table and the incense in the room that her mother had been praying to her spirit goddess, Myal.

Dominique noticed the disapproving look in her daughter's eyes. "I am praying to Myal for peace. I am praying for serenity. I am praying for healing."

"All well and good, Mother. But physically, how are you? Let me take a look." Angeline stood closer to her mom and looked at the welt on her eye and her cut lip.

"The bruises and cut will heal and so will my shoulder which was injured when he threw me on the table," Dominique said. "Did you find out anything in Portsmouth?"

"Yes, let me tell you. But I will be brief. The police ignored our complaint but with the help of Jacob Harlow and his son, Michael, we were able to make contact with someone who said he can track down Javel and deliver justice."

"The police ignored you?" asked Dominique. She began to cry.

"Mother, we will find the man. We will," stated Angeline, trying to stem her mother's tears.

"Who is we?" asked Dominique, wiping her face with the hem of her dress.

"Michael Harlow, Jacob Harlow's son. The two of us went to an apothecary named Quigley who took us to see the leader of the Jamaicans in Portsmouth, a man named Sobadu. Sobadu said he will find Javel."

"What did you say his name was?"

"Sobadu."

The look on Dominique's face was one of fright, then wonder, and finally a fierce scowl of anger.

"Mother, you look frightened. What did I say?"

"If it was the same Sobadu I knew in Jamaica, then I know this man. Tell me, what did he look like?"

"He is a black Jamaican, stands over six-feet tall. Taller than most men."

"How old is he would you guess?" Dominique's voice held an edge of urgency.

"Late forties, maybe fifty years old."

"That must be him. I do know him," Dominique sighed. "There can be only one Sobadu. I thought he was dead, killed in the rebellion in Jamaica."

"If it's the same man, he is very much alive. We were told that the Jamaicans in Portsmouth fear him. He is some sort of witch doctor."

"He is an Obeah man," said Dominique, getting up from her kneeling position next to her altar to Myal. "He conjures up the forces of evil and vengeance. He is Jamaican. I am surprised he is alive. And even more surprised he is in Portsmouth."

"You never told me about Obeah. You pray to Myal. She is a Jamaican goddess of peace and harmony, right?"

"Yes, she is." Dominique had been careful about what she told Angeline about her past in Jamaica. She had kept many secrets from her daughter. But if Angeline was going to face Sobadu, she should know what she was up against. Dominique hated him.

"He is very dangerous, Angeline. In Jamaica, he was the son and grandson of Obeah men. They taught him many things about Jamaican magic herbs, drugs, potions. These Obeah men think they can dream up the spirits to control others, not only in their minds but in their physical bodies. They pretend to heal, they pretend to predict the future. They pretend to help so they can receive favors in the future. I knew this man, Angeline. He will do anything for power. But he is a fake. He uses drugs and poisons to manipulate his followers. He can take the heart of a pufferfish and use it as poison. He will cut the head off a chicken and use its blood as a magic potion."

"But we were told the Jamaicans in Portsmouth obey him, even fear him."

"I don't doubt that," said Dominique. She turned from Angeline and put out the candles on her makeshift altar. "I do not doubt that."

"He said he can bring in Javel. Give you justice."

"Bring in Javel?"

"Yes, he said if we were to go to the Kent Street warehouse next Sunday with some new sheets as payment, that he would have Javel. You would have to identify him, and the other Jamaicans that will be there would pronounce sentence on Javel for what he did to you."

"I could be in great danger if I were to see Sobadu," said

Dominique. "But he could be in great danger as well. I hate him so much. I have carried this hatred for twelve years."

"Why do you hate him? What did he do?"

"I cannot tell you, my sweet baby, Angeline. My sweet baby." Dominique took her hands and placed them warmly on each side of Angeline's face. "There are some things you cannot know. There are some things I cannot tell you. I must live with them."

"Then you must go and confront Javel. You must go, Mother. Otherwise our efforts will have been in vain. If he can be caught and punished, even if it is by this Obeah man, then you will get your justice. Your revenge."

"Myal has been telling me in my dreams that revenge is a two-edged sword. You may hurt the other person but you harm yourself when you seek revenge. You must understand that Myal teaches me to forget if not forgive. Sometimes she works for me. Sometimes she doesn't."

"Certainly, you must go," pleaded Angeline. "Javel might hurt you again. You alone know what he is capable of doing."

Dominique thought about what Angeline had just said. She could be in danger from this man in the future. "You're right, I'll go with you. Javel took more than my dignity when he attacked me. He took my self-respect. I was never innocent before this. That was gone long ago. But he took my sense of safety in my own house. He made me fearful for me and for you. Safety is important for me and for you to live here. Yes. I will go with you and we will see Javel. We will see Sobadu, if only to make sure he is the same man I knew in Jamaica. But I will take a knife with me, and you should do the same. If there is a confrontation, and there may be, you should be armed."

Angeline had never seen her mother so ruthless. She had never thought of her mother wielding a knife in anger.

But of course, my mom is tough. She defended herself against Javel with the spiked cotton carder.

The look in her mother's eyes made her feel exactly like she had felt when she kicked that thug who had tried to pull her out of the pub. There was something "like mother like daughter" in that look.

◆ ◆ ◆

When Monday morning came, they knew they had a long work day ahead of them. Angeline thought of the production they needed. They needed to get Eli Williams his eighteen sheets. They needed to make ten more for Sobadu by next Sunday. They needed help. Even if one of them or the other worked the loom for twelve hours a day for six days, they wouldn't get the quota done alone.

Angeline made a quick decision as the sun broke over the horizon, and she went next door to ask Agnes Fairfield if she would help them weave. Thank goodness, Mrs. Fairfield said yes. It would cost them a half-shilling a day or three shillings for the week. Agnes could spin the yarn just as well as Dominique and help set the loom with thread.

When Agnes came over, Angeline told Dominique that she had to go see Eli Williams at the hospital and explain what happened and that they might fall short of their requirement this week. She knew they couldn't physically produce twenty-eight, six-yard-long sheets in a week. She ran the half-mile to the hospital.

After she caught her breath from the run, Eli's secretary, Mrs. Hewitt led Angeline into Eli Williams' office in front of others who had early morning appointments. There were many vendors to a huge operation like Haslar which could have as many as one thousand patients at any given time.

Angeline filled Dr. Williams in on her journey to Portsmouth and the attempt to find someone who could bring Javel to justice.

"This Sobadu witch doctor is demanding new sheets from us as payment since I told him Mother and I were weavers."

"How many?" asked Eli.

"Ten sheets. We don't have any inventory so we will have to make them this week before Sunday," decried Angeline. "Agnes Fairfield will help us, but it means that we will only be able to bring you either eight or ten sheets by Saturday. I need to delay bringing them by a day and bring at least eight fewer than I normally give you. I hope you will understand. We will make up the difference next week."

"That should be fine, Angeline. I do hope you and Dominique will find who did this. Don't worry about the sheets. I'll alert the nursing matron. If we run out, I'll get a message to Henry Pennington."

"Henry Pennington?" asked Angeline, worried. She remembered hearing his name and how he'd wanted to supply sheets to Haslar Hospital.

"Oh, don't worry. He has a shop across the bay. He's always wanted to supply cotton sheets to the hospital. If I need extra sheets, I'll call on him, but don't worry, his bid is too high, and you have the work as long as you want."

"Thanks, Doctor. I have to run. We have a busy week ahead of us."

◆ ◆ ◆

On the other side of the bay, near the Baffin Pond marsh, Sobadu and Slash were ankle deep in water, combing the reeds for certain plants. They had been in the ditches. They had been in the woods to the east. They had been on the outside of the sea wall, combing the narrow beach. It had been a busy day, starting early in the morning. Since it was getting late, they needed some last minute catches before retiring back into the city.

They had been looking for plants, herbs, and flowers. Sobadu valued the herbs for medicines. He valued others as potential poisons. They found some of what he needed in the ditches, and some in the land surrounding dung-rich livestock enclosures. Since it was late July, the growths they wanted would be in full bloom. It was an intense and active hunt.

Slash didn't know what to look for unless Sobadu told him. They both carried huge burlap bags which by now were stuffed with the various plants and reeds they had collected.

Some of what he collected would be used in his Sunday rituals. Some he would trade with Quigley for oils and tinctures and exotic poisons that could only be obtained from LongAcre Supply in London. These included poisonous plants like foxglove, and oleander that Quigley could purchase from them. Sobadu thought it was a curse that LongAcre was unwilling to deal with him not only since he was black but also a former slave.

In the marsh, both Sobadu and Slash were getting wet on purpose. Sobadu had done this before but it was infrequent. He had a small net in his hand so he could capture newts, small salamanders. He wanted as many as they could net and take home live. In this part of the world, they would be active in the early evening. They were normally found in marshes as they moved from the land to the shallow waters and back again.

Certain parts of the salamanders' bodies were lethal poison. Poison of the strongest variety. He didn't want to go through Quigley to ask for the poison from LongAcre. Too many suspicious minds might take notice.

He had created poisons like this a few times in the Caribbean with pufferfish. That was twenty years ago when his father and aging grandfather showed him what to do. Although weaker in concentration than pufferfish, he found out that the newts worked as well.

When the two of them had what they needed, they made their way back in the early evening to a room that Sobadu could use. This was a room that only Slash and Sobadu knew about. In it, he had bags and vials of herbs and poisons he had collected and could obtain at a moment's notice. He never slept here. The room was under lock and key that only he could open.

The two of them sorted the herbs and flowers, laid them to dry on the floor, and left the newts in the bag until each was ready for processing.

Once the herbs and other flowers had been arranged to dry, Sobadu went to work on the newts. He grabbed one at a time and brought it to his work table. For the entire evening, by candlelight, he dissected them to extract the poison.

He was very careful preparing the poison. He put on thin layered gloves and a paper mask over his nose and mouth. Then he would bisect the heart and liver and squeeze the toxins into a vial.

The toxin he extracted was a powerful nerve poison thousands of times more toxic than deadly cyanide. He had used it on some murderers in the Portsmouth area. The Jamaicans had come to him for justice, and if the crowd wanted death for the murderer, he delivered the toxin into the man or woman and the effects would be certain.

The poison would usually manifest itself in five to ten minutes. The victim would feel numbness, headaches, rapid heartbeat, seizures, and soon after, respiratory arrest and death. He had witnessed death occurring in as little as twenty minutes, but in another case, it had taken longer.

There was a reason he used poison to kill the men and women who the crowd had said deserved killing for their crimes. With poison of this exotic nature, the white power structure—the police in particular—would never be able to prove how a certain person died, if they cared at all to inquire.

Most times, with the kind of power that the mayor had given him, it was obvious they didn't care what happened to a black man or woman. They didn't care what happened to them when the Jamaicans were slaves and they didn't care now that they were free.

Once he had finished with the newts, he tossed the remains into a garbage pail and took inventory of the herbs he had available. He knew his standing in the Jamaican community was as an enforcer of justice but also as a healer. That reputation only grew if he had herbal medicine that did some good. In this way, his people could rely on him and avoid the white English medicine which they distrusted. The more he was able to cure their minor ills, the less they trusted the English. The less they trusted the British, the stronger Obeah would be in their lives. Everything was working in his favor.

He glanced at the rack on the wall that held passionflower oil that he would use as a sedative for headaches and for burns. The wild lettuce was drying on the floor. He and Slash had picked it for its milky juice or latex that he squeezed out. It was also used as a sedative. Sometimes, if there was enough, he would give it as a mild narcotic that helped with insomnia or muscle pain.

He and Slash had collected as much jimsonweed as possible. It was also called devil's snare or devil's weed. Sobadu had long used its leaves and seeds to cause hallucinations. It was perfect for his Sunday ritual. It had a long history of ceremonial use. He normally used it as incense, never wanting anyone to eat the leaves or the seeds. Concentrated use of it a few years ago proved to be fatal.

In the summer heat, the devil's weed leaves had to be stripped from the plant and left to dry. He collected what seeds there were to burn in a large pot during the ritual or to place a single seed in a blunt of tobacco during the ritual.

The two of them had been able to harvest copious amounts of salvia, the hallucinogenic plant that he prepared for the Sunday rituals.

One poison that he had to obtain from Quigley was the calabar bean or chopping nut. In Africa, Sobadu's ancestors used it as a trial or ordeal poison. Individuals accused of witchcraft would drink the white, milky extract of the bean, made by crushing the bean in a mortar and soaking the remains in water. If the accused died, it was considered proof of their use of witchcraft. If they lived, usually due to vomiting up the poison, then they were declared innocent and set free.

He also obtained abrin from Quigley. Sobadu was afraid of using it, even touching its poison, because a single seed could be fatal. Quigley had shown Sobadu the rosary pea which contained the abrin in its seeds. The seeds were red with a black spot covering one end. If the coating of the seed was broken, as little as the poison in one pea seed could kill.

As a practitioner of Obeah, Sobadu was well versed in poisons and other harmful substances. Many Africans killed themselves in Jamaica rather than suffer at the hands of the plantation owners.

Sobadu's father, grandfather, and he himself had provided the necessary poisons for those who wanted to die. It was a ghastly event to watch someone suffer from one of these poisons, but they did what was asked. Hundreds of deaths during the days of slavery were attributed to poisons devised by Obeah-men.

At the end of the evening near midnight, he finished his ritualistic preparations of herbal medicines and poisons by intoning an Obeah prayer to Legba, the most important spirit in the hierarchy of Obeah.

> Oh, Legba you are the intermediary between all living things and the spiritual world.
>
> I pray to you.
>
> I ask you to bring power to these herbs so I can heal—and if it is your will—to end someone's earthly life and send them to you.
>
> Papa Legba, I have prepared herbs and plants to please you.
>
> I ask your permission to use them in your name.

When his small prayer was finished, Sobadu was too tired to go and find another place to bed down for the night. He had been in the habit for ten years of knocking on a single woman's door and inviting himself into her room for the night. Instead he pulled a blanket from the closet, spread it out, inhaled deeply of the remnants of herbal incense in the room, curled up, turned out the last candle, and went to sleep dreaming of the marshes of Portsmouth.

CHAPTER 10

GOSPORT

They had worked the spinning wheel and the loom for 12 hours a day for five straight days. Saturday morning, as she had promised, Angeline was able to deliver ten fresh cotton sheets to the hospital. She waited with her receipt slip that the orderly had signed for Mrs. Hewitt to bring her £3 for the sheets from petty cash. Angeline was exhausted as was her mother and the neighbor lady, Agnes Fairfield, who had been a godsend, helping as she did for those five days. Even now, early Saturday morning, Agnes was at the weaving shed helping Dominique finish the ten sheets that they had to bring to Sobadu the very next day.

After Mrs. Hewitt gave her the money, Angeline jogged back to the weaving shed. The three women knew that despite how hard they worked, the capability of the small four-poster loom and their spinning apparatus just couldn't be pushed any faster than it had been the past five days. *One more long day*, thought Angeline, *and we should make it*.

"But I only gave Haslar Hospital a couple more than half their normal weekly order. We will have to work hard next week just to catch up if that's even possible," muttered Angeline to herself. This payment to Sobadu was a big one. It had harmed their ability to serve their main customer. Yes, they could afford it in a sense, because of the good graces of Dr. Williams. But Angeline worried that if they fell behind, Eli would be forced to ask Henry Pennington to supply what he needed and alas, once this man got his foot in the door, he might be able to take over the business and shove Angeline and her mother to the gutter.

All day Saturday, the three women worked to complete the ten cotton sheets. It was a struggle, but they were able to do it.

◆ ◆ ◆

Sunday morning came after a restless night for Angeline. Sobadu had put fear into her heart, which kept her from sleeping well. He had blatantly tried to scare Michael. His physical presence and his bullying attitude gave her pause as to whether she had done the right thing by contacting him. Now she had to see it through.

As Angeline and Dominique got ready to go to Portsmouth, they went to the kitchen and each grabbed a knife from the cutlery set. They looked at each other as they slipped the knives into their waistbands. That look in their eyes revealed both apprehension and resoluteness. Neither knew what was going to happen. Dominique had not told Angeline why she hated Sobadu, and that troubled Angeline. It continued to bother her as they walked to the ferry dock and boarded the single-mast sloop that would carry them across the bay. Sharing the burden, each carried five sets of the sheets.

After the two of them had disembarked from Victor Jerdan's ferry, they walked to Jacob Harlow's brokerage office where they were met by Jacob and Michael. After they greeted each other, Michael spoke. "I took the time this morning and scouted the warehouse where we are supposed to meet Sobadu."

"That's why you didn't go to church services with me?" asked Jacob with a tone of disapproval in his voice.

Michael didn't respond to the criticism. "Now that I know where it is, we can make a plan as to how to approach this. I can tell you that the warehouse will be filled with Jamaicans this afternoon."

"That's when we're expected to be there," said Angeline.

Dominique remained silent but was aware that she would soon be the center of attention.

"The way I see it, Sobadu will bring Javel out at the beginning of his Sunday ritual and get the business over and done with," said Michael. "I don't see him wanting to wait to get his crowd riled up to deal with this. I don't know what he does in these Sunday rituals, but I don't think it's anything we should stick around for. My dad has agreed to wait at the ferry docks and help get you both boarded on the ferry so you can get back tonight. He has a pistol. Let's hope he doesn't have to use it. They won't let me in the warehouse, but I'll be outside and provide a sort of rear guard in case anyone hassles you or tries to follow you back to the docks. Inside, you two are on your own. At the first sign of trouble bolt for the door. Are either of you armed?"

Michael's tone was commanding, insistent, and it made Dominique worried. Angeline was worried as well.

"We both have knives," said Angeline. As worried as they were, they had asked for justice from a man who had a brutal reputation. They had been forced by a lazy or corrupt police force to seek this man out. They had to deal with it. There was no backing out.

"We have a few hours," said Jacob. "Please, come to our house and you can eat something before you have to go to the docks. It's a few blocks from here, but not too far. After your meeting is over, if your exit to the docks is blocked, you can stay at the house overnight."

◆ ◆ ◆

When Angeline and Dominique arrived at the warehouse, sheets in hand, they were halted by Slash, his machete in a sheathe tied to his waist.

"Stop here," he ordered. Then he turned abruptly, opened a door, and disappeared. Angeline put her hand to her waist and touched the hilt of the knife. She wasn't sure if her mother could fend off an attack with a knife, but she would do whatever she had to do to defend the two of them. While Slash was gone, she turned to see

Michael hiding in an adjacent alleyway across the street. He was tucked behind a barrel, and only acknowledged his presence to her with a low whistle.

Slash came back to the women as abruptly as he had left. "Follow me," he said. He took the sheets from them and led them to the front of the warehouse. Near to them were twenty or thirty Jamaican men. Some were sitting, some were standing. Angeline could hear drumbeats as the men started thumping the homemade Jamaican drums. She could smell incense in the air. On a warm summer late afternoon in a cotton and tobacco warehouse, there was scarcely enough air to breathe. No windows or doors were open. She felt choked by the stuffy, herb-laden air. She turned to see if her mother was all right. "How do you feel?" Angeline whispered.

"I can barely breathe," said Dominique. "Let's get this over with."

Although it was light outside at four in the afternoon, there was scant light in the room with all the warehouse doors closed. In the dim light, Angeline could see a black man tied and trussed up to a post with a gag stuffed into his mouth. He was bleeding from cuts above both eyes, and his mouth was bleeding as well.

"Mother, look over there. Is that Javel tied up?" whispered Angeline.

"Yes, that's him," answered Dominique. "Although with all the blood on his face, I can't be sure in this dim light. Angeline..." Dominique's voice shook. "I'm frightened. I want to leave."

"Ha, ha, ha, not so fast! You won't be leaving here for a while!" boomed Sobadu, sounding cheerful. He had entered from a hidden room, so he stood behind them.

The two women turned sharply around to see Sobadu in full costume—the hat, the cape, the white talc painted on his face. He also had a woven bag strapped to his waist. He was just as big as Dominique remembered him from the jungles of Jamaica.

Sobadu looked at Dominique and she at him. There was instant recognition. Despite the fact they hadn't seen each other for twelve years, there was no mistaking Sobadu. She took a step or two backwards away from him.

"Sobadu! It is you!" said Dominique, reeling unsteadily. Although it was large, the closed-in feeling of the room, made her unsteady on her feet. She wanted to sit but couldn't. There were no chairs anywhere.

"And Dominique, there you are. Sweet Dominique, after all these years we meet in Portsmouth," said Sobadu with a sneer on his lip. "What a chance meeting, don't you think? I bet you never thought you would see me again. Thank you for the sheets. They will suit me quite nicely."

Dominique wrung her hands. "I thought you were dead."

"As you can see, I am very much alive," snapped Sobadu.

Angeline saw that her mother was unsteady and blurted out, "You said you could bring justice for her attacker."

"In good time, Angeline, my young and insistent friend."

"I am not your friend. I am a customer. You got your sheets, now give us what we paid for."

He gave Angeline a look that made her shiver. "You are demanding, my child. Demanding to a fault. Do not make Sobadu angry," barked Sobadu. "First, we establish a few things."

"Like what?" replied Angeline, trying to sound strong.

"Dominique come with me," said Sobadu. "You too, Angeline."

Slash followed the two women behind Sobadu who led them to the man tied to the pole.

Sobadu ripped the gag from the man's mouth so Dominique could get a good look at his face. Even though the man had been beaten and had dried blood above both eyes, and a bloody lip, she could see the man's ripped cheek. It matched perfectly the marks made by the spikes of the cotton carder. A shudder went through her body as she was face to face with the brute who'd tried to rape her.

"Just to be sure, where did this attack take place?" asked Sobadu.

"In the weaving shed next to our house," replied Dominique.

"There are many houses in Gosport. Where is your house?" insisted Sobadu.

"I don't know why that is necessary," barked Dominique. After a pause and a glare at Sobadu, she said, "It's on Maiden Lane."

"Is this the man who attacked you?" asked Sobadu.

"Yes, that's Javel. The pig!" said Dominique as she slapped the defenseless man across his face.

"Is that the justice you crave?" said Sobadu with a patronizing grin. "A slap on the face. If that is all, I'll untie him and let him go. He already bears the marks of Slash's fists when he resisted the attempts to catch him."

"No!" yelled Dominique, now starting to sweat under what was a stultifying, herbal-infested air that she was forced to breathe. "I want justice."

Sobadu turned from her and raised his hand to the crowd of men who suspended the beating of the drums. They crowded closer to the three of them. Slash kept a watchful eye. He did not move as the crowd inched toward Sobadu but kept his hand on his machete.

"I will ask my Jamaican brothers what they think is just punishment. You know of course, sweet Dominique, that if we untie Javel and let him go after a mere slap, that he will probably hunt you down and kill you, most likely in a brutal way."

"Kill him, then!" shouted Angeline.

"Be careful what you ask for, Angeline. My, my, you are a hot-headed one, aren't you," snapped Sobadu. "Temper, temper."

Sobadu addressed the crowd pointing to Javel. "This man has been identified as the man who beat Dominique and attempted to rape her. He did not succeed. I ask you, what is proper justice? The offended woman, Dominique, wants more than a slap on the face. Her daughter wants the man killed. We can set him free. We could brand him on his cheek with an M for malefactor as the British courts would do. We could kill him. The only thing that I will say for him, acting as prosecutor, barrister for the defense, and judge, is that the victim is still alive and breathing, although not well at the moment. If we let Javel go, he will hunt this woman down and harm her, even murder her. We would do her a big favor if she didn't have to worry about him for the rest of her life. What say you? A slap, a brand, freedom, or death?!"

Regardless of what the crowd decided, Sobadu was sure what he was going to do, but he was going to extract something in the bargain.

"Dominique, come with me. Angeline stay here. Your mother and I have something to talk about."

Angeline protested and started to walk with her mother.

Slash took three steps and stood in front of Angeline to stop her.

"Mother! Don't go with him," cried Angeline.

"Myal will keep me safe," said Dominique as she caressed the crystal she wore around her neck. "I have lit many candles in her name. She will protect me."

Seeing what her mom was doing, Angeline also moved her own crystal in her hand, saying a small prayer to whatever god that existed to help her. She didn't care if it was the Christian God or Myal. She didn't want to see her mother harmed. All she could think about was that this had been a terrible idea. She should have never insisted on seeing this witch doctor. They could have walked the streets and killed Javel on their own. This was madness.

Sobadu and Dominique stood looking at each other in a small room adjacent to the main warehouse hall.

"How did you escape Jamaica?" asked Sobadu.

"Ran to the hills, to Santa Maria, where we were caught and sold to a Scottish plantation owner who brought us to England. And you?"

"I escaped like you when the Jamaican maroons came to hunt down Tacky. Was shipped to England on a slave ship, same as you."

"How come you weren't killed like my husband Tacky?"

"Tacky was not your husband. He was the father of your child and many others. He had three mistresses, one of whom was you. You were not married."

"To me, he was my husband. You should be dead like him, shot by the British authorities or by their lackeys, the maroons. You and your 'fairy dust' that you sprinkled on the men who rebelled with Tacky. What a mistake. You are not an Obeah man, you are a charlatan! You ran into the arms of the maroons who were sworn to hunt us down!"

"I did not do what you say."

"You are a liar and a coward!" Dominique had been harboring this hatred for years. She blurted out her accusation venomously.

"Careful with your language. I hold the power of life and death in this part of the city. The mayor and his friends have given me this. People can disappear from this warehouse and never be found again, and the white men don't care."

"Are you threatening me?"

"Just stating a fact, my sweet Dominique. Just stating a fact. I have great power. You should respect that. Look what I have been able to do for you. I have caught Javel. Brought him to you. If I let him go, he will eventually kill you. Is that what you want?"

"I know your secret, Sobadu. I know what you did. If I tell your people, you will lose your power in an instant. They will no longer think you are a great Obeah man. They will know you as you are— a coward." And she spat on the ground.

"No. You won't," Sobadu said. He hesitated as he considered what he was going to bargain. This one person may know why he was still alive after the rebellion in Jamaica that killed its leader Tacky. Whether she knew what he did or not was the question he had to ask himself.

"Shut up! Listen carefully. I will put it to you simply. Do you want me to let him go, free to hunt you down? Well do you?" Sobadu let his voice grow louder than hers.

"No," answered Dominique losing control of her already frayed emotions. "I want him dead. I want you dead!"

"Here is a bargain. I will only kill Javel if you promise for all time to keep silent about my past in Jamaica. If you don't agree to this, I will let him go free. My price for this justice is your silence."

Dominique thought to herself as she turned from Sobadu and walked to the other side of the small room. *If I say yes, I will never get revenge for Tacky's death. Javel will be gone, but so will my ability to hold anything over this fake Obeah man. If I say no, Javel will kill me or Angeline. Or maybe Sobadu will have me killed. I must protect Angeline.*

Dominique turned and faced Sobadu. She looked him straight in the eye and told him her decision. "You have my word. I will never speak to another person of what happened in Jamaica. You will own my silence. Hold it close to you. Hold it close to what passes for your heart."

"A wise decision, Dominique, a smart choice. You must know that this is a bargain now between us. A lifelong promise between us. No one, not even your daughter will know of this."

"I said I will never speak of what happened in Jamaica to another living soul."

The two of them rejoined the warehouse group. Sobadu wanted to regain control of the room. He knew that the flock, his parishioners, would be edgy. He needed to start the incense, get the Sunday ritual started that they expected.

"Beat the drums loudly," he commanded. Ten of the members present went back to their drums and started beating them as loud as they could.

He turned to Slash. "Bring Javel in front of everyone."

When Javel was untied from the post, Slash held him with a rope tied to his hands that stretched between his legs. Slash stood behind Javel ready to yank the rope should Javel try to run.

In a loud voice, Sobadu commanded that Javel kneel in front of the crowd. The drums were loud and insistent.

"You have been identified by your victim, Javel. She says you are the man who assaulted her. She says you beat her and attempted to force yourself onto her. You say you did not do this." And then turning to the crowd, he shouted rhetorically, "Who do you believe?!"

His request was greeted with silence. No one spoke.

"None of them can really say. So your trial, Javel, has been established. Someone bring me a mug of rum for Javel."

One of the congregation brought him a crude clay jar with a small amount of rum. Sobadu reached into the woven bag tied around his waist and pulled out a small vial of crushed calabar bean. Sobadu tipped the vial carefully and poured some of it into the rum right in front of Javel's face.

"Your punishment, Javel, is in the form of a wager. You will drink the extract of the calabar bean in this rum. If you live, you will be declared innocent and set free. If not, you will be dead and declared guilty.

"Hold his head back," shouted Sobadu. Two men held Javel by the shoulders, another forced his mouth open. Sobadu poured the liquid down Javel's throat and then pinched his nose and mouth together to force him to swallow the liquid.

Within minutes, with more than fifty people watching, Javel showed signs of the poison. He was kneeling with his hands tied behind him. His entire body began to twitch spasmodically. His head and face were sweating, and his chest heaved up and down as his breathing became irregular. He tried to get a full breath which never came. After two full minutes of this ordeal, the seizures stopped, and his heart stopped as well. He fell to the ground dead.

"He must have been guilty!" yelled Sobadu. Not wanting the death of Javel to mesmerize the crowd, he regained control of the audience. "We shall celebrate Obeah's law. Celebrate the great Obeah. Beat the drums louder."

As the Jamaicans started to get rowdy, eager to start their Sunday drinking, smoking, and dancing ritual, Angeline and Dominique exchanged glances and took a couple of steps toward the door.

"Stop!" yelled Sobadu. "Javel will never be seen again. He will never be found. You have your justice. You have what you wanted. You may go. But, Dominique, you remember our bargain. You remember what I said."

They met Michael outside and the three of them walked quickly to the docks where Jacob Harlow waited for them. Michael followed from the warehouse. The women were anxious to put this entre event behind them. They were unsettled by what they had just witnessed. In a way, they felt relieved that Javel was dead but there was also guilt and shame for having been accomplices in a man's murder.

As they approached the ferry boat dock, Michael ran ahead of them and said to his father, "They're here."

"God be praised," said Jacob exhaling deeply. "God be praised."

As Michael helped the women get into the ferry, Michael turned to see a single black man standing twenty-five feet away and looking intently at them. "Do you know that guy?" asked Michael.

"He's one of Sobadu's henchmen," said Dominique. "I saw him in the warehouse. Probably making sure we're leaving."

Dominique and Angeline told Michael and Jacob the entire story of what had transpired, and of Javel's death. As the two women got aboard, and Jacob and Michael helped push Jerdan's boat away from the dock, Jacob said, "It's Sobadu's territory. In his part of Portsmouth, he can get away with murder."

CHAPTER 11

GOSPORT

Dominique and Angeline sat quietly during the boat ride across the bay. It was a beautiful summer evening and the breeze off the Solent powered Victor Jerdan's ferry and washed some of their anxiety away. Neither of them spoke. Both women were alone in their thoughts. Dominique had been angry and eventually frightened by what Sobadu had done. It wasn't going to be easy to get over it.

For her part, Angeline was relieved that the evil Javel was not going to be a threat to anyone ever again. She understood that if Sobadu had let him go free, the two of them would be looking over their shoulder for him whether they were in Gosport or Portsmouth. Javel's death was something that had to be done.

Angeline was different than her mother. Physically, she bore a slight facial resemblance to her father, although her eyes and high cheekbones reflected her mother's attractive looks. Angeline was slightly taller and stronger than Dominique, and it was obvious as she matured into adulthood that she was driven to achieve. She didn't know what it was inside her, but she felt that she was destined for things that were bigger than weaving cotton sheets day after tiring day.

She could see the distress in her mom's face on the ferry boat ride back to Gosport. The entire ordeal had weighed heavily on her. She needed rest more than Angeline did. Coming face to face to Sobadu—the death of Javel right in front of them—was traumatic for her. Her Myal was not a vengeful deity. Myal was harmony. Myal was peace. This entire sequence of events starting with Javel's attack shook her deeply.

As she thought about the differences between herself and her mother, Angeline realized she was probably more like her father, Tacky. As a five-year-old, she never really knew him as anyone other than a leader of a rebellion. Beyond that, her mother never spoke much of him.

Her mother wanted peace and harmony and a non-stressful existence after all she had gone through escaping in Jamaica to Santa Maria. She suffered through protecting Angeline while she was running away from a certain death during the rebellion.

She protected me from all harm during those difficult events, thought Angeline. *That we were sold to the Stewarts was a bit of good fortune. The years with them as household servants was a lot easier than working in the cane fields. I was told the brutality of the overseers was merciless. Mother knew that many Jamaican slaves killed themselves with poison rather than submit to the harsh treatment. Traveling across the Atlantic Ocean was an ordeal only to be sold to Duncan and Franks at Haslar Hospital. That couldn't have been easy for Mother, even though we had been able to live in rooms at Dr. Duncan's house. It was not without its difficulties.* She could understand why her mother wanted a peaceful life as a free woman in England.

Dominique would not be able to curb Angeline's angry spirit. Her praying to Myal did not work. She could light all the candles she wanted to. She could pray to her goddess. But her mother would never understand why Angeline felt the need for action, achievement, even power. Those feelings had to be more like her father, even though he was but a distant memory. She was but a young girl in Jamaica and he was rarely around them. He was either in the fields or in someone else's shack at night. But she was told that this man was her father and that he'd once been a chieftain in Africa, before being captured and sold to planters on "Sugar Cane" island.

◆◆◆

It was a slow walk from the ferry dock to Maiden Lane. When they arrived home and were eating some warmed-up peas and potato stew at their dining table, Angeline felt compelled to ask what happened with Sobadu.

"What went on between the two of you when Sobadu and you spoke in secret?" asked Angeline softly, trying not to agitate Dominique. Having been through an afternoon and early evening of confrontation, fear, and the death of Javel, Dominique's nerves were on edge.

"I can't tell you, Angeline, my sweet Angeline," said Dominique. "I swore not to tell anyone."

"Not tell them what?" inquired Angeline, still keeping a quiet tone of voice.

"Just what I said. I gave him my word that I would not tell anyone, including you. It's best that you don't know. You want to live, don't you? You don't want him hounding you, stalking you, killing you? Well, do you?" Dominique put her head down on the table in mental and psychological exhaustion muttering so low that Angeline couldn't hear clearly what she said. "I may be the only one in England who knows what Sobadu did."

"I didn't hear what you said, Mother. Please?"

"No, Angeline, no. What I know could ruin him and he knows it."

"Knows what?' Angeline was starting to get more insistent.

"He killed Javel right in front of us because I swore not to tell anyone about what he did in Jamaica. In return, we got our revenge. I got my revenge. It was my decision. Now you must be kept safe from Sobadu."

Angeline replied, "I can keep that secret. But if I know, then your mind will be at ease. You can be at peace. Don't just hold this in. Can't you see? By doing this, he has made you a prisoner. You are chained to the power he has over you. You want to protect me. I want to protect you. Tell me."

"No. No. No. Just stop." Dominique quickly rose and went to a window. In the distance, she could see the water channel that led to the Solent roughly a quarter of a mile away.

"You cannot know. You cannot," stressed Dominique. "It's getting late and we have a work day ahead of us. Please, don't ask anymore. Let's get some sleep. If you smell incense, please don't come into my room. I must pray to Myal tonight. I must pray for our safety—your safety."

Dominique and Angeline went to their separate rooms. Angeline went straight to sleep, but Dominique set up her little altar to Myal, and lit a few candles and burned some incense. She wanted some of the Solent's sea air, and opened her window as wide as she could.

She went to her small trunk in which she had all her earthly possessions and pulled out a small diary. In it were prayers to her mythical goddess that she'd written over the years. She could only write small amounts in English. She only wrote what was important to her. These prayers had been penned over a ten-year span. She read one of them softly to herself.

> Oh Myal, goddess of healing,
> oppose this evil that has been done.
> Forgive me my sins.
> Cleanse me.
> Obeah evil has been done and I am responsible.
> The guilt is mine.
> Forgive me.
> Bring your joyful spirit to me.
> Bring your goodness.
> Let me sleep in peace.
> For you are the temple of holiness

You are the holiness of that temple.
You are my mother.
I was conceived in your womb.
I live in the womb of Myal, holy Mother,
Make my daughter Angeline safe.
Always safe and secure.
For I believe in you.
I believe in your power.

Dominique sat for a moment with the spirit of her prayers running through her heart, giving her comfort. She thought about her confrontation with Sobadu. She thought about his maniacal need for power. She thought about the danger he put her in. She knew once again, she had to do something to protect Angeline. With the strength of Myal governing her thoughts and her hand, she took a crude pencil she had in her trunk and wrote in the diary for the next hour.

◆ ◆ ◆

It was Sunday night after the ritual in the warehouse. Sobadu sat alone that evening in the rough rooms of one of the Jamaicans. The windows were open, and Sobadu could feel the light summer breeze. He started to think about the evening's events in the warehouse. He thought about what he had done and whether he had enhanced his power with the Jamaicans under his patronage. What he didn't have to worry about was the fate of Javel.

"No one will ever find Javel," he muttered to himself. Like others who had met the same fate, Javel was being unceremoniously carted to a small dory at the docks. Under the camouflage of darkness, Slash and another man whom he had recruited had hauled Javel's body to the dory boat, loaded heavy rocks into the legs of his pants, and tied them off at the ankles so the rocks would be contained. The two of them rowed the body out to the east of Portsmouth about a half-mile off the coast and dumped it into the Solent. It wasn't the first time Sobadu had gotten away with murder and it wouldn't be the last.

"There wasn't a single person in the mayor's office on down, including the police that would care if Javel was killed and buried at sea," whispered Sobadu to himself.

As Sobadu sat and rested on the bed awaiting the return of Slash to report on the "burial," he thought about what Dominique had said with all the venom she had for him.

"I know what you did, Sobadu," Dominique's voice kept ringing in his ears. "If I tell your people what you did, you will lose your power. They will no longer think of you as a great man!"

He was troubled by it. It was true, and Dominique was the only person in England who knew his Jamaican history. And since she was one of Tacky's mistresses, she might actually know what had happened.

He went over the life he had in Jamaica, his short-lived escape, capture, and his shipment to England. He was lucky they didn't hang him. The slave ship was terrible. Rats wouldn't have lived in those conditions. But the slaves did. It was rough but he had managed to convince the captain that he had the power and the herbs to sedate the slaves and make the captain's voyage smoother. It was a stroke of luck that other slave ship captains had known of Sobadu's Obeah power. At the captain's direction, the first mate had purchased a large quantity of the needed herbs in Santa Maria. *Yes, it worked. I was able to put the herbs to good use and I wasn't in a hold and chained 24 hours a day. God, that ship smelled like death.*

As he lay there for over two hours, he finally decided he had to do something. He had executed Javel. He had accepted Dominique's promise not to tell. But did she really know? And what good was that promise? What good would that promise be if she could save her life by telling someone? If she told someone, would it matter? Would people believe a poor weaver from across the bay? Who would she tell? The Police? Cady or Varlo? No. They wouldn't listen. Why would they care? *As long as they get what they want, I can do whatever I want. They wouldn't care about my past. What if she told Slash? Would it matter to him? He had a well-paid job. Very well paid. Better than slinging bales of cotton at the docks or scraping lumber dregs from the hull of a new ship's keel. He is a quiet, sordid lot, he is. It just comes back to me in my thoughts time and again that I shouldn't take any chances. No, it's stronger than that. I can't take any chances. No matter if Dominique promised that she wouldn't tell, if she had to save her own skin, she would. There is only one way to ensure that I get to keep my power in Portsmouth. Dominique must die.*

Sobadu drifted off to sleep until it was almost midnight when Slash knocked on the door. No one else but Slash knew where he was, so Sobadu could safely assume it was him at the door.

"Come in," said Sobadu immediately waking up. "Close the door behind you. Did you dump the body in the bay?"

"Yes. With large rocks in his pants, just like before." said Slash.

"Go home and sleep," said Sobadu slyly. "I might have a job for you tomorrow. I'll pay you extra for this job."

CHAPTER 12

PORTSMOUTH

The murderous plan came to Sobadu in front of his only candle the night before. It would be a perfect execution. He stared at the candle burning a long time before he snuffed it out. Killing people like Javel with a calabar bean solution would not work for this. But the juice from his poisonous newts' hearts and livers would.

Slash had found Delroy and had made him watch Sobadu's room all night. Sobadu always wanted someone to be in the hallway so no one could sneak up on him. At times, he had other men who guarded him, but Delroy was chosen this night so Slash could get some sleep.

When Sobadu woke, he opened the door to the hallway to see Delroy asleep.

"Delroy!" Sobadu shouted. "Wake up!"

Delroy's eyes opened when he saw Sobadu standing over him. He immediately got to his feet.

"If you are selected to guard me, don't fall asleep!" barked Sobadu. "Do I make myself clear!"

"Yes, yes, Sobadu. I'm sorry. It won't happen again."

"If it does, you could find yourself buried in the swamp. Are you awake enough to listen to what I want you to do?"

"Yes, yes."

Sobadu needed a few things from Quigley's apothecary before he could carry out his plans. "Here is a shilling. Go to the apothecary and tell Quigley to fetch six long stem, hardened, thick candles and candle wick fiber—a long string of it. Stay there while he gets them and bring them to Slash. He will know where to find me. You got that Delroy?"

"Yes, candles and candle wick fiber," said Delroy.

When Delroy left, Sobadu packed up what little he had with him, and as stealthily as possible, crept down the stairs and went to a room a few blocks away. This was the room that could only be opened with a key that he had. It was the room that contained all his vials, potions, oils, and poisons. Slash would know to go there.

When Sobadu arrived at his storeroom, he opened the door, set his small pack on the ground, and looked up on his shelves for the necessary tools to accomplish the task that would take most of the day. It was late in the morning, but he thought he could get everything done by six or seven that evening.

He set out several items on a small table: a scraping tool, some gloves, a sharp blade, and a bowl he would use to apply the poison.

An hour or so later, Slash knocked on the door and identified himself with a telltale grunt. Sobadu let him in.

"Do you have the candles?" asked Sobadu.

He recognized them immediately in Slash's hand and took them from him. Sobadu examined the two-inch diameter candles and said, "They have to stand on their own."

He placed one of them on a table to make sure it wouldn't tip over. It was thick enough so it didn't fall over. "These should do."

For the next fifteen minutes, Sobadu instructed Slash as to the exact operation that Slash was to perform, where he was to go, and the reward he would get for this murder.

"Take the ferry over to Gosport and locate the house on Maiden Lane where Dominique and Angeline live. Disguise yourself so no one recognizes you. Locate the house in reference to the road from the hospital because that's the way we will be coming from. If you can, determine which room is Dominique's. You have seven hours or so. That should give you plenty of time to get back here."

The operation was not that involved, but it needed some scouting. Sobadu wanted Slash to know every step so he didn't fail. Slash had killed for Sobadu before, usually with his machete or another blade. But this time, there could be no mistakes and no blood. He could not abide failure. "If it fails," said Sobadu. "We may never have a second chance. Now go. Be back at seven."

After Slash left, Sobadu locked the door and went to work. He wanted to do this work in the daytime to use the most light possible. He couldn't afford a single slip. Spilling anything could cost him his life, and it would not be an easy death. Poison could harm the perpetrator as well as the victim.

He had to wear gloves. If he got any of the poison on his hands, arms, face, or on any skin, he would suffer a horrible death alone.

The gloves he pulled from a chest of his personal possessions were tight fitting men's knitted silk gloves, probably Italian, lined in plain ivory linen. Where he had stolen them from was a distant memory.

He found the sharpest knife he owned, placed it on the table, and laid out the candles lengthwise before him. He stretched out the cotton fiber and cut lengths of it that matched the lengths of the wicks in the candles. Then he placed a bowl at the far end of the table, out of the way of his elbow. "No spills," he kept saying to himself. "No spills." He didn't want to breathe any of the poison. He put a cloth over his face and tied it around the back of his head.

With this preparation, he took his knife and carefully cut lengthwise through the first candle to its center to expose the wick. He had to use some pressure to slice through to the center of the candle. He then used the knife to clean out the tallow that was in the narrow knife groove. Then he took the blade and widened the channel ever so slightly so that he could remove the candle's pre-set wick and so he could place one of his own in the channel. He was very careful with the cuts he made in all five candles.

Now for the dangerous part. He got up from the table and retrieved the newt heart and liver poison. He opened the vial and gently placed the liquid in the bowl in front of him. He was breathing rapidly by this time.

He took the first piece of cotton fiber and delicately placed it in the bowl so it could soak up some of the newt poison. He watched the cotton fiber expand as it absorbed the substance. He had left an end of the cotton fiber string hanging over the bowl so he could grab it. When he could see that the fiber was fully saturated, he pinched the new wick between his index finger and thumb, lifted it from the bowl, careful not to drip any of the poison onto the table, and placed it lengthwise into the channel of the first candle.

He followed the exact steps for each of the remaining candles save one. It was warm in this room, and the window was closed to keep any breeze from disrupting his "lab work."

He had just enough poison in the bowl to saturate five candle wicks. He felt successful that he had been able to get the cotton fiber wicks placed inside the channels of the candles that he had dug out.

To complete the job, he lit a non-poisoned candle, and keeping his mask and gloves on all the time, took the wax from the burning candle and dripped it in the channels, sealing the new wicks. This process went smoothly but very slowly and took valuable time. It took the burning of an entire candle and a few hours in the afternoon to finish. He hoped that the wax-cooling, sealing process would be finished in time.

◆ ◆ ◆

Slash showed up and knocked on Sobadu's door around seven. The sun was just starting to set with sunset scheduled for around nine p.m. The skies were partly cloudy with a waning moon, so he didn't have to worry about a full moon shedding light where it wasn't wanted. The attack had to be in the dark of night, deep into the night. The least light the better. Both Sobadu and Slash needed to be hidden.

"Did you find the house?" asked Sobadu.

"Yes," replied Slash. Slash never spoke much. He had learned over the past ten years that Sobadu only wanted results and didn't care for any other explanations.

"Were you seen by anyone?"

"No."

"Can you find it in the dark?"

"Easily."

"I am going with you. I'll help row and steer the dory. Listen carefully. Take this small vial of opium and this rag. You'll need them. I've put the candles and matches in this woven pouch. I'll give it to you when we get to Gosport. Stay here until it's dark, then we'll leave. Sleep if you can."

◆ ◆ ◆

The two of them pushed off from shore around eleven at night, with both Slash and Sobadu rowing. They went out from Southsea and headed up the shoreline close to Portsmouth. They didn't want to venture too far out into the open Solent or the bay until they had to. They had kept the boat in the marshes and avoided the commercial traffic that was normally docked up the shoreline close to the warehouses. It was going to be a rough row into the wind.

Sobadu knew that they would have to row past Ft. Moncton that stood guard to the Portsmouth bay. To avoid detection, he took old torn linens with them to the marshes and previously tied them around the oar paddles. It wasn't perfect, but it helped to muffle the sound of the oars in the water.

By Sobadu's rough calculations, it would take them the better part of two hours to row across the bay and land far away from the Gosport ferry dock and near the westernmost edge of the Haslar Hospital cemetery.

It was a warm summer night with only a slight breeze out of the west. It would slow down their approach, but hasten their return.

Sobadu only had to give Slash his instructions but once. Slash had all the necessary gifts to be an assassin. He was short of normal height by a couple of inches, but his sinewy strength and agility combined with a malicious heart made him a formidable killer.

Having been abandoned by his parents, Slash grew up in a hateful Portsmouth orphanage, and over the past twenty years spent his life on the streets. It was his stealth and escape artistry that had kept him from the noose or Bridewell prison.

He always planned his escapes even to the number of steps and body position he needed to avoid being spotted or imprisoned. Ever since he murdered the orphanage matron who had caned him regularly, he hadn't felt anything when he knifed or garroted someone. He was good at both. He worked without extra noise and escaped the murder scene the same way. Silence was a perfect companion.

It was close to one o'clock when they docked the dory on the gravel beach. Sobadu gave Slash the pouch with the candles with his instructions. "There will be an open window. Enter through the window, put the opium on the rag, then stuff it in her nose to knock her out. Be sure she is unconscious before you leave her side. Light the candles. No one must see you do this. Be quick about it. There is another larger rag in the pouch. Use it to cover your mouth. You don't want to breathe the fumes. At all. Close the window on your way out. Be quiet. She will never wake up."

It was the middle of the night as Slash walked the half-mile to Maiden Lane. When he arrived at the house, he could see a small candlelight in the room he assumed was Dominique's. The candle burning was for Dominique's evening prayers to Myal.

Slash stayed outside the open window and could smell the tallow burning of Domonique's candle. He wasn't going to hurry. He listened carefully. The only sound was from crickets chirping in the night and the sound of the soft breeze off the Solent rustling through the tips of the treetops.

Slowly, he reached his head up to the windowsill and peeked in. Dominique was in bed. She probably let the candle burn itself out in the night. This was good for him. He would have some light to help him enter.

The window was opened just wide enough for Slash to reach the top sash and carefully, slowly, push it up so he could crawl in. His small size and his agility made this an easy entry. He took the rag and opium from the pouch and crept to Dominique's bed. He doused the rag with the opiate, and pressured it against her mouth and nose, covering them forcefully.

He looked at her eyes as he grabbed her and held her against the bed. She tried to struggle against his body weight, but the amount of opium that Sobadu had given Slash was enough to knock out two people, much less this diminutive woman.

Dominique stopped struggling and Slash saw that her eyes glazed over and then shut tight. He held the cloth to her mouth for another full two minutes before releasing it.

He removed the rag, placed it back in his pouch, then removed the candles and the other rag. He tied the larger rag around his mouth, placed the candles on the small altar to Myal that Dominique used, and used the flame from her candle to light the ones he had brought. He was as quick as he could be, not wanting to breathe any of the fumes.

Slash left through the window, shut it quietly, and jogged back to the boat. Sobadu was waiting on the shore, and the two of them manned the oars for the first couple hundred yards as they made their way with a following wind back to Portsmouth and safety.

◆ ◆ ◆

Dominique's respiratory arrest came in stages. Knocked out by the opium, she was unaware of the initial changes to her body. Since there were five burning candles and the window was closed, there was rapid onset of the effect of the toxin. Within fifteen minutes, her tongue, nose and lips felt a prickly and tingling sensation. Then the same crawling, itching feeling engulfed her face, fingers, toes, and arms. As the poison entered her lungs, her breathing became labored, she started sweating, and she couldn't move her legs.

Immobilized, she woke up just long enough to feel the rapid weakening and paralysis of all her muscles, even her voice box. She couldn't yell and couldn't move as the respiratory attack, abnormal heart rhythm, and seizure led to her death.

Her life ended in less than forty-five minutes.

CHAPTER 13

GOSPORT

The sun came up in the east just like any other day. But this morning was completely different than any other morning. Although Angeline's room was on the western side of the house, she could tell that the sun had risen because of the blue sky and the sharp shadows in the backyard adjacent to the weaving shed.

Angeline was usually the second to rise and normally would find Dominique at the kitchen table with tea and her breakfast. When she wasn't there, Angeline paused a moment to listen to the sounds in the house. Perhaps her mother was in her bedroom getting dressed. She heard nothing.

Angeline went to her mother's door and knocked. "Mother, are you up?"

There was no response.

"Mother," she said a bit louder. "Are you awake? Time to get up."

There was nothing but silence.

Angeline opened the door and immediately recoiled against the stuffy room and awful, foul smell. She ran to the window and shoved it open and said as she faced outside and took a deep breath, "You usually have the window open, Mother—" and turned to see Dominique lying in bed, her upturned face distorted and flushed.

117

There was vomit on her face and chest, her tongue bloodied from trying to chew it off in agony, and her entire body was contorted as she seemed to have struggled to escape from her own skin. Aside from her tongue, there was no blood anywhere.

"Mother!!" cried Angeline. "Mother!! Wake up! Wake up!" She shook Dominique who was like a limp doll in her arms. Angeline put her ear to Dominique's face to see if she could detect any breathing. There was none. She tried to feel her pulse at her wrist. There was none.

"Oh God, no!" she yelled. "No. No. It can't be!"

Confused, frightened, and shaking, her knees twitching so much she could barely stand, Angeline tried to think. *What caused this? Was there someone in the house? Was I in any danger?*

She ran out her mother's bedroom door, scurried into the kitchen to grab a knife, and tore upstairs. Breathing heavily, ready to slash the person who had done this, she saw nothing. Her mind racing, she made her way downstairs and out into the back yard. Nothing.

"This can't be! It can't be! No! No! No!" Angeline cried aloud. She needed help. She needed someone to help her.

She went out to the weaving shed and found the two Gosport women, Agnes Fairfield and her friend Dana—who helped them with the weaving—were just settling into their work.

"Something terrible has happened to Dominique," Angeline blurted out. "I have to get help. Oh, please, Agnes, Dana, I fear my mother died last night. I have to go and get help at the hospital. Please do what you can here. When I find out anything, I will tell you. If you would please do what you can on the loom today? Don't go into the house. I will see to what needs to be done. Please."

With that short request, Angeline cried uncontrollably. She ran out into the yard and cried aloud to no one in particular, the tears running down her cheeks, "You didn't keep her safe, Myal! You fake! You fake! She prayed to you morning, noon and night! She prayed for her safety. She prayed for my safety. Look at what's happened to her. You fake!"

Angeline ran as fast as she could to Haslar Hospital. She covered that half-mile in five minutes. As she ran closer, she saw the guards at the gate, and Willie Ferris standing next to his transport carriage chatting with one of the guards.

"Willie!" Angeline yelled. "Willie!" she yelled once again.

Willie turned towards her as she came to the gates. She was panting heavily. She leaned over, put her hands on her knees, and caught her breath enough so she could speak.

"Willie, something terrible has happened. I found my mother dead in bed this morning. Please I need someone's help. Please!"

Willie put a hand on her shoulder. "Go inside and tell Eli Williams, Angeline. I'll stay here. See if you can get him to release a couple of the guards to help you with her body," said Willie.

"She isn't even cold yet. Damn it. She died last night when I was asleep. I don't know what to do. I don't know how it happened!"

"Just go in and tell Eli, he will help," replied Willie, trying to remain calm. "I'll stay here."

Angeline rushed up the walkway, through the doors, and up the stairs to Eli Williams' office. Mrs. Hewitt was at her desk.

"Mrs. Hewitt, I need to speak to Eli. My mother is dead. I found her this morning!"

"Oh my God," said Mrs. Hewitt rising quickly from her desk. "Wait here, I'll tell Dr. Williams you're here."

"I don't know how any of this happened!" said Angeline.

Dr. Eli Williams met her at the door to his office. Mrs. Hewitt stood nearby. "She wasn't breathing, she had no pulse. She wouldn't wake up," Angeline said painfully. "I need help. Please help me," she cried.

"We need to take a look. But I can't go. They're setting up a surgery for me in ten minutes. Let me think… I'll send Dr. Foreman over to check out the body," Eli said sternly, changing rapidly from a concerned friend to a surgeon with a mission to perform.

"Can you send some guards back with me as well?" said Angeline. "Willie Ferris said he'd drive everyone in his carriage."

"Certainly. Mrs. Hewitt, send an orderly to fetch Dr. Foreman, tell him it's a medical case and he'll need to bring his medical bag. And tell the chief of the guards to send two of his men with Dr. Foreman."

"Will do, Dr. Williams," replied Mrs. Hewitt as she rushed quickly and called over an orderly who was posted near the administrator's office as an internal messenger within the large multi-ward hospital.

"I am so sorry, Angeline," said Eli. "So sorry. I wish I could come with you. I only have a few minutes… Let's allow Dr. Foreman to decide what's best once he has seen Dominique. My God, I am so sorry that she died. Any idea what caused it?"

"None. I know nothing," cried Angeline. The two of them left with Eli locking the office door behind him. He walked to surgery and she went out the front door to wait for Dr. Foreman.

Dr. Dan Foreman had been at Haslar Hospital for two years. He was a friend of Dr. Jim Hawkins and Dr. McLaughlin before they had moved to Bristol. He had been fresh out of the Royal Medical College at Edinburgh and had been a friend to Angeline and Dominique over the past two years when Hawkins was still in Gosport and the two women had worked for him.

After assigning ward duties to the chief matron, Foreman came down with his medical kit to the waiting coach parked in front of the hospital gate. Rather than overload the single-horse rig, the two guards said they would jog briskly to Angeline's house leaving Dr. Foreman and Angeline in the cab as Willie drove. During the short ride to the house, Foreman tried to get some preliminary information.

"I am terribly sorry to hear of your mother's death, Angeline. I really liked Dominique. She seemed so kind and generous. Do you have any idea what happened?"

"Thank you, Doctor," replied Angeline. "I don't know how she died. She worked so hard. So hard. I hope it wasn't a heart attack. She was young."

"How old was she?" inquired Foreman.

"Mid-thirties, I would guess. She had me when she was only a teenager."

"Tell me anything you can, Angeline," said Foreman, pressing the issue as they arrived at the house. "Anything at all about what you saw, what you heard, what the room smelled like."

"The window was closed. She usually left it open at night… to get the breeze of the Solent, she'd say. That was different."

"That does sound unusual, given that it's summer," conjectured Foreman. As they came to the house, Foreman said, "Let's go in and have a look."

The two of them entered the house and went straight to Dominique's bedroom. When they went into the room, Foreman walked over to the body, and looked at Dominique's head, feet, fingers, and hands for any signs of a struggle or defensive wounds of any kind. He took his time, his movements slow and careful. He looked under her fingertips for any skin from an attacker. There was nothing under her fingernails, but they were a soft purple color as were her lips. He looked at her neck and hands. He spent most of his time around her face. He had taken a small spoon from his medical box and scooped the vomit away from her mouth and put it in a vial while Angeline stood a few feet away and started to weep softly.

"What did you do that for?" asked Angeline.

"I don't see any visible reason why she died, Angeline. There is the reddening of her face, but I want to look at the vomit for anything she might have ingested. If you permit me, I also want to take a sample of her blood and look at it under the microscope at the hospital. When Dr. Hawkins and Dr. McLaughlin were here, they had secured a microscope from Scotland and we have been collecting specimens ever since. We can compare Dominique's blood with some others that we have on slides. There might be a clue there as to why she died without any visible signs."

"Go ahead if you want to," said Angeline wiping her face with one of her mother's towels and holding it close to her face for a minute or longer. A baby will always know her mother's smell, and although Angeline was almost eighteen, she could smell her mother on the towel. It was comforting but also extremely sorrowful.

It took Dan Foreman a minute or two to get his needle ready but when it was, he poked Dominique's arm and extracted a vial full of her blood.

"What are we going to do now?" asked Angeline.

"Well, I think we should have these two guards wrap Dominique in a sheet and take her to the hospital where we can take a look at her. I can't tell you what to do, but I suggest she should be buried at the hospital since there is the cemetery there. Will you want a church service?" asked Dan Foreman as gently as he could.

"Church service? See the small altar she has set up here against the window? Yes, over there next to the burned-out candles. There you will see her church," replied Angeline.

"I don't understand," said Foreman.

"Her church didn't have spires or pews or any stained-glass windows, Dr. Foreman. Her church was in nature. She was a believer in Myal, an Afro-Jamaican goddess who brought her some sympathy, some peace and some… safety," Angeline started crying again.

Angeline stopped weeping long enough to say, "We'll have a service at the cemetery when you're done examining her, Doctor. I'll say some of her prayers. She would like that. Maybe I'll even add some of my own."

The guards came into the room, and with Angeline watching, picked up her mother's corpse, wrapped her body in her sheets, and carried it out to the waiting carriage. Willie hadn't wanted to come in to see Dominique dead in her bed. Not only was he a bit sheepish about the dead, but he had seen too much death and the agony it brought to families. He could see the anguish on Angeline's face as she came out with Foreman and the guards knowing he could do nothing to relieve her grief.

Willie drove the entire entourage back to Haslar. The guards managed to hang onto the outside railings while Foreman and Dominique's corpse were inside. As they drove away, Willie could see Angeline staring at the carriage as it pulled out of sight.

Angeline went to the weaving shed and spoke briefly with Agnes and Dana. They were working at the spinning apparatus and the loom. Angeline was still in a state of shock. Her words came out slowly and hesitantly as she tried to collect her thoughts.

"The doctors will examine my mother's body to see if they can figure out what happened. Ah… in the meantime, I want you to continue working, if you can, please. I will have some things to do. I don't know exactly but… well… anyway… I need to be away from this. You two are in charge of this operation. Get as many sheets to Eli Williams as you can manage. I just don't think I can help you right now. Take the sheets you have on Friday afternoon to him as usual. I fully intend to compensate you for the extra work. We'll work something out."

Angeline abruptly turned from the two women and walked outside. She was embarrassed at showing them her tears. They would understand, of course, but Angeline didn't want to appear as weak as she felt, not at that moment, anyway.

When she entered the house, she walked back to her mother's room. Was it too early to put her mother's things in a closet? Was it sacrilegious to move her things so quickly after her passing?

I'm at a complete loss. I have never done this before. I don't know what to do. At least I can find some prayers to say at her graveyard service. Prayers to her Myal seem appropriate. My Christian prayers—the Our Father—will ring hollow. My mother did "forgive sins done against her. She was a forgiving person. Why would she die like this? Where is your magic now Myal?

All of Angeline's confusion about religion and what it was supposed to accomplish seemed like so much nonsense. It couldn't bring her mother back from the dead. *Dead is dead. What the hell can some God do about it?*

Angeline opened Dominique's chest and pulled out her prayers that had been written many years ago. She leafed through them and picked one or two out that would be right for her mother. As she knelt down to look for others, she saw a letter with her own name on it. *To Angeline* it read on the envelope. Angeline opened the envelope and read the disturbing note that Dominique must have written after they had arrived back from their awful meeting with Sobadu. The letter's penmanship was barely readable.

Dear Angeline,

I don't know when you are reading this. We had that meeting with Sobadu. Do you remember. He took me into a room where only he and I could talk. You could not come in. Remember? In order to have that brute Javel killed, I had to agree to keep a secret that if revealed would ruin Sobadu's power with the Jamaicans in Portsmouth.

This is the secret. This is what happened. When your father Tacky, my husband, started the rebellion in Jamaica, they did some terrible things. You and I were sent away with our belongings to escape to the North. Tacky and his men were falsely anointed against harm with Sobadu's "fairy dust." I knew he was a fake. He knew I hated him. What he did during the rebellion was evil.

The maroons were blacks given their freedom by the British if they would capture rebels. Tacky was a rebel. He was a chief. In order to save his own skin and get free passage to Santa Maria and to England, Sobadu told the maroons where Tacky could be found. They found him, and they killed him. All with Sobadu's help. Sobadu killed my Tacky, killed your father.

Angeline folded the letter and sat down on her mother's bed to think. *I could kill Sobadu for what he did to my father. He will answer for that. My mother was too kind. But she was also afraid of him. That's why she insisted on taking a weapon to the meeting with him.*

Angeline wanted to tidy up the room before she would take the letter to Eli Williams and Dr. Foreman. She needed advice from those who had some authority. As she leaned over to pick the items that made up her mother's altar to Myal, she saw the burnt wax from five candles, the remains of which were different than the candles Dominique had usually used in her prayer sessions. She picked up some of the wax and held it to her nose. She turned her head away in disgust as the putrid smell entered her nostrils. She thought it was the same smell that was in the room when she entered the room a couple hours earlier. It seemed different than the smell Dominique's normal candles produced.

Angeline wondered what it was, and rather than scrape the burnt wax up and toss it into a garbage can, she fetched a small woven bag and put the wax shavings and a few of the remaining wicks in it to carry to Dr. Foreman. Maybe he could tell what it was.

◆ ◆ ◆

"I can't tell you what to do with this letter, Angeline," said Eli Williams after he read the painful last thoughts of Dominique, whose body was undergoing an autopsy at the hands of Dan Foreman. "These events happened how many years ago?"

"Ten or more, Dr. Williams," responded Angeline, still in a confused state. "It is certainly my mother's words against Sobadu's. He will clearly deny what she wrote here, but I believe her."

"I am inclined to believe her as well. I know something of Sobadu, but not much. According to the doctors here at Haslar who live in Portsmouth, Sobadu has increased his control over the blacks of Buckland since he's been here. The doctors have spoken of him, but I have not dealt with him at all."

"If he knew that my mother wrote this… if he knew that my mother knew of his treachery… he could be the one who had her killed," barked Angeline. Her temper was getting the best of her, and she had to be careful not to explode in front of Dr. Williams. He had been generous with her and her mother, and she didn't want her emotions to ruin her relationship with him.

"You don't know how your mother died, Angeline. Don't jump to conclusions without evidence," countered Williams.

"Isn't this letter evidence?"

"It's an allegation of wrongdoing, ten or more years ago. There's no proof," said Williams.

"I have these burnt wax shavings that I took from Dominique's altar. I don't know what they are. Would it be all right if I took them to Dr. Foreman and asked him to test them to see what they're made of? I mean the candles could be poisonous."

"Poisoned candles? You are stretching for something, Angeline. Let me look at them." Williams held the shavings close to his nose and took a deep breath.

"Well, they don't smell exactly like normal tallow candles. Tell you what, I'll see that they get to Dr. Foreman. He's taking a look at her vomit he collected—what her stomach contents reveal. He can test Dominique's blood. This would be additional evidence but perhaps the shavings will tell us something. But, please don't get your hopes up. This is going to take time and I can't spare him from his wards for more than an hour or two at a time."

"When do you think her body will be ready for burial?" asked Angeline.

"Day after tomorrow at the earliest. I'll send a message to you when we are done with her remains. It depends on how long Dr. Foreman wants her for examination. So you go home and rest, Angeline. You've been through a lot."

Angeline went back to the house but couldn't sit still. She wrote a short note explaining what had happened, took some money, and went straight for the ferry dock. She gave the money to Victor Jerdan and asked him to find a messenger in Portsmouth on his next trip and give it to Jacob and Michael Harlow.

CHAPTER 14

HASLAR HOSPITAL CEMETERY

Angeline held a small posy of flowers that she had picked from her mother's garden and looked around at the small circle of mourners at the burial ceremony. Agnes Fairfield and Dana, Dr. Eli Williams, Dr. Dan Foreman, Willie Ferris, and Jacob and Michael Harlow were all standing respectfully around the gravesite. It was an unusual scene. Normally when a sailor who died at Haslar Hospital was buried, the only people who were in the vicinity were two gravediggers.

It had been two days since Dominique had died. Angeline received a short note only the day before that Eli Williams would release the body for burial. Angeline immediately ran a note to the Gosport docks where Victor Jerdan could make a late day ferry ride to Portsmouth to get the message to the Harlows.

Angeline was glad Jacob and Michael had been able to come. They had dropped all their business activity and arrived early in the morning after taking Jerdan's earliest return ferry ride to Gosport.

Agnes and Dana had been kind enough to take some money Angeline had given them and purchased some food from Gosport's only food purveyor for a small gathering after the ceremony.

Angeline was not the domestic sort, but she did the best she could to prepare some food and drink.

The short service started around noon. The gravediggers had opened a small shallow plot and had placed Dominique's linen-wrapped corpse in it. All that was left was to cover the plot with the sod and dirt that had been removed. All the graves in Haslar cemetery were shallow because of the water table from the adjacent Solent river.

Angeline knew she should say something as the small group gathered.

"Thanks to all of you for coming. My mother was a loving, caring woman who sacrificed a great deal to be here in England. She was especially kind to me even though as I grew up, I was not kind to her. She protected me against all kinds of danger, on sea, on land, in Jamaica, and in England. I regret that I was often angry with her as I grew up. That was changing over the past year as we worked together at the loom. 'We have to get along,' she would say. 'Otherwise we'll never succeed.' She was right. I will offer some prayers from the Christian bible that would be suitable as we lay her to rest, but she was not a Christian. So I will leave those for later. She was a strong believer in Myal, an African-Jamaican goddess of harmony. I found this prayer she had written. Mama, please rest in peace for all eternity." Angeline could barely read the prayer through her tears.

> I invoke the spirit of Myal. I offer you a prayer of thankfulness. Please listen to my prayer.
> Oh Myal, you have given me a child. I thank you.
> You have kept us safe. I thank you.
> You have protected us. Thank you.
> I will do what you wish.
> We will do what you wish.
> Oh Myal,
> You are my church.
> But there is no life without Myal.

To you I bow.
I will pray to you.
Protect me for all eternity.
I pray for your kindness.

Angeline wiped her eyes and continued haltingly, "I have a few words from my Christian bible to add. I wrote them down so I would not forget them. And Jesus said, *Let not your hearts be troubled. Believe in God; believe also in me. In my Father's house are many rooms. If it were not so, would I have told you that I go to prepare a place for you? And if I go and prepare a place for you, I will come again and will take you to myself, that where I am you may be also.*"

With this, Angeline could not hold back here tears. She could barely finish what she wanted to say. "Oh Mother, please find rest. You didn't deserve to die so soon. You had so many years left. I will miss you." And with that Angeline tossed the flower bouquet into the grave. There was silence as Angeline nodded to the gravediggers to begin filling the dirt back onto of the linen-covered body of Dominique.

As the gravediggers finished their work, Angeline said, "Agnes and Dana have prepared some lunch for anyone who wants to come back to the house. Doctors, I know you are busy so I will understand if you can't join us. Willie has agreed to give a ride to those who want one. It's not a long way and I'm going to walk back. Thanks to you all once again."

The group disbanded and Agnes, Dana, and the Harlows went with Willie. Eli Williams came to Angeline, expressed his condolences, and then left to go back to his office saying, "Dr. Foreman will share his results with you, Angeline."

Dr. Foreman lingered to talk with Angeline. "Let's walk for a bit, shall we," he said. The two of them walked through the cemetery towards the hospital gate.

"What have you found, Doctor?"

"Call me Dan, will you. I'll leave the formal title for the hospital staff. I've only begun, Angeline. I just don't have much time. I did what I could before today, because I knew that Eli had told you that you needed to bury your mother, so I did what I could. I was able to look at her stomach contents and the vomit to see if she had ingested anything poisonous. I didn't turn up anything. Nothing appeared out of the ordinary. If she had eaten something poisonous, it might have showed up."

"What about the wax from the candles?"

"That was interesting, but nothing conclusive. Yes, the wax smelled differently than other candles. I took the small amount of wicks that were left and I have kept them. I haven't had the time to look at them or the blood under the microscope. In fact, if I may be honest with you, it could take weeks of full-time effort to compare the scrapings of the wick, the candle wax, and the blood samples and compare them to slides that we have accumulated from different diseased sailors. It's a big chore. We don't have the staff or the time."

"I could do it. Just show me how to use the microscope."

"Angeline, you have had no training in what to look for. You need Dr. McLaughlin. He brought the microscope here. He collected and classified the slides. He knows what he's looking for."

"He's in Bristol with Jim Hawkins," lamented Angeline. "That's three to four days ride by coach… both ways. I don't have the time to get him. Show me how to use it. I can work the loom in the mornings and use the microscope in the afternoons if you show me how to use it. I promise to be careful."

"I know you would be, but the two Robertson microscopes we have here are in constant use. Ever since the microscopes were brought here by Dr. Mclaughlin, we use them in many ways. Under his guidance before he left, he started a system of keeping very good records that help in making comparisons."

Foreman paused and looked at Angeline and the sorrowful look she bore. "I'll tell you what. I'll get it cleared with Eli. You come over tomorrow afternoon, say around one o'clock. But I warn you, it may take weeks."

Angeline walked back to her house feeling confused and sad.

She really couldn't think straight. When she arrived, she didn't want to talk to anyone. She was emotionally addled, her brain and heart ripped open to reveal that of a young woman whose life was turned upside down. Both Agnes and Dana tried to get her to eat something, but she couldn't. The Harlows and Willie Ferris both saw the distress on Angeline's face and thought the best thing for them to do was to go back to Portsmouth.

"Angeline, I know this is difficult for you and we are so sorry," Jacob said. Jacob had lost his wife and knew how devastating it was to lose someone close to you. He remembered his own mental state and how the thought of mixing with other people was so distasteful even though they were friends.

"Michael and I are going to leave, but if there is anything you need, please call on us," said Jacob quietly.

"Yes," added Michael. "When you're feeling up to it, come over and we'll share what we all know about this terrible tragedy and how it may have happened."

"Thank you both," said Angeline sincerely. "I'll do that. But right now, I can't even think. Willie, would you be so kind and drive the Harlows to the ferry dock. Feel free to come back and eat with us. We want to share all this food."

"I'll do just that, Angeline. I'll be back soon," said Willie, and the three men left somberly.

◆ ◆ ◆

Dan Foreman and Angeline were in the lab the following afternoon. Both were sitting next to one another at a lab table with the microscope in front of them. Foreman started his instruction. "It's more than just focusing on a tissue or blood sample. It's recognizing what it is that you see. Comparing your sample to a good sample, or a sample of another patient that has a particular disease is where the real analysis comes into play. I've prepared slides with Dominique's blood, and slides with really small pieces of the wax and slivers of the remaining candle wicks we had. This microscope is a marvelous invention and a godsend. This microscope will enlarge the image up to fifty times."

Angeline was eager to get going. She had spent the morning weaving sheets and had turned the process over to Dana and Agnes. Angeline told them that they would get their pay raised if they took responsibility for meeting the sheet quota for the week. Angeline had to offer that incentive because she was under pressure to get Eli's sheets to him. She feared if they came up short too many times, Eli would have to bring in Pennington, and that could spell the end to their income. Angeline had to help in the mornings. She could only spare afternoons and evenings. But her biggest problem in viewing the slides that Dan Foreman brought to her was the amount of light.

"This mirror at the base of the microscope reflects light back up under the slide you are looking at. As you can see from the large windows with sun coming in from the south by southwest, the afternoons are the best opportunity for the best light. Since I've been here, it has been suggested to light a candle under the microscope to get light at night, but the fear of losing slide material was too great. So, Angeline, forget about looking at slides at night. You have to be efficient in your use of the sunlight while you have it. When you look at the slides you will have to decide quickly if a slide compares to Dominique's and move on. We have a thousand for you to look at.

"A thousand slides?" exclaimed Angeline.

"Oh yes. McLaughlin set up the organization for them and we have followed his protocol. But yes, we have collected blood samples from every sailor who has been here for the past three years."

"And I have to look at every one and compare it to my mother's blood sample."

Angeline looked up and examined the slide of her mother's blood. "That's all I have that's left of her."

"The ones from Haslar's sailors are in the drawers to your right. Each of these has a small card attached to the slide that describe the sailor's problems, if he died here, and where his disease may have come from. Each has a number. When you take one out of the filing cabinet box, be sure to replace it correctly. We don't want them mixed up."

"It seems overwhelming," said an exasperated Angeline. She wondered if she could ever find anything that would determine how her mother died.

"I'll set you up and look at a couple of them, but then I really must get back to the wards I supervise. This hospital currently has 890 patients, all with various diseases or injuries that need attention. The Admiralty finished this hospital at the end of the French and Indian wars, or what we Brits call the Seven Years war, to take care of the needs of its wounded. They tell us that we should expect more if a war breaks out with the American colonies."

"How do I use it?" asked Angeline. She was not interested in history other than her own and that of her deceased mother.

"First, here is some paper, pen, and ink. If you see one that compares favorably to your mother's, write down the slide number. Then I'll look at them and verify what you've found, okay?"

The microscope looked like a foreign contraption. Angeline had never seen one before, but she was anxious to get going.

Foreman told Angeline how to work the microscope and completed the actions as he said them. "Place a slide from the cabinet onto the small plate, like this. Look into the lens and adjust the mirror so you have the best possible light reflecting upwards. Then look into the lens with one eye closed. Then, adjust the coarse focus knob until you have the information on the slide in focus. Then use the fine focus knob, that's this one here, and easily, slowly turn the knob until the slide is in focus again. Now you try. Go through the steps."

Angeline did as she was instructed. It took a few tries to get one eye focused on the material on the slide. But after doing a few, she started to feel comfortable with the protocol that she had to follow. As the light coming through the windows changed minute by minute, adjusting the reflecting mirror became a necessary step for each slide.

Dan Foreman was ready to leave but left her with some vital tips. "Don't rush. You have to slow down your thinking and concentrate on what the microscope is showing you. Using a microscope correctly is one part concentration of one's eyesight and one part trying to understand and articulate what you're seeing. You have to get used to the uncertainty when you see something for the first time under a microscope. Unsettling, isn't it? I'll check back with you in a couple of hours. See how you're doing. The best thing you can do is to find some that compare favorably to your mother's. Oh, and Angeline…"

"What's that?" said Angeline as she rearranged her chair to be right in front of the microscope on the table.

"Don't jump to conclusions. You'll lose valuable time and get frustrated. That won't help. Patience is the word to remember."

Angeline would be hard pressed to be patient. It wasn't one of her virtues.

With Foreman gone, Angeline got busy. She took each slide from the Haslar drawer, placed it under the slide, and looked at it. She tried to grasp what it looked like, then put her mom's slide on the tray to compare it. It was eerie to think that she was looking at what was left from her mother—a bit of her blood on a slide. She tried to get over that and concentrate as Dr. Foreman had said.

She had to readjust the mirror each time she put a slide on the tray. With her concentration on the light from the windows, she could tell that the sun was setting even though with each slide, the movement of the mirror was slight.

The laborious part of this work was focusing and concentrating. It was entirely too easy to let her mind wander and sometimes see things that weren't really there. Often with each sailor's slides she could imagine what she wanted to see when she would put one under the microscope, focus the lens, then stare at the blotches and splotches that made up a sample, then put her mother's up for a quick comparison. She had to put her mother's blood sample slide up often, as many as two or three times for each of the sailors' slides just so she could be relatively certain that there was no match.

Sailors had come from all parts of the world to Haslar Hospital. The English ruled the seas in the 1700s having won their wars with the French and the Spanish. The notes that accompanied the sailors' slides at Haslar Hospital notated diseases from as far away as the Far East, India, Africa, and the Caribbean. The notes said that they had died from scurvy, which Angeline did not understand at all, malaria, sleeping sickness, alcoholism, rotten pork, rotten beef, and the largest cause of all, infections from battle wounds.

As Angeline went through about twenty-five slides in the first hour, she felt her concentration, eyesight, and attention span diminishing. None of the slides she looked at had any faint resemblance to her mother's. Her mother's blood sample on the slide had distinct markings. She let her imagination get the best of her a few times and was ready to see things that weren't really there, and write down a number for Dr. Foreman to look at when he came back. But more often, she didn't feel confident at all that the slide compared to her mother's and replaced it in the drawer.

Luck was not on her side her first afternoon. She didn't see anything to write down. Dr. Foreman had cautioned her against moving too fast and jumping to conclusions. "All right," she mumbled to herself, "I won't, but there has to be something. One of these sailors must have been poisoned!"

♦ ♦ ♦

It was the fourth day of examining the slides of dead men. It was the fourth day of constantly placing her mother's blood sample slide back on the microscope tray to see if there were any similarities. She hadn't written down one single slide number on the paper Dr. Foreman had given her. Then she saw something on the slide from a sailor who had come from the Caribbean.

She put the slide on the tray, looked at it carefully, and then moved it off and looked at her mother's. There was something. There was a similarity between the two blotches of blood on the slides. She picked up the card that accompanied the slide. She had read so many, maybe hundreds by this time, that she didn't expect to read anything of value, yet there it was. The card read, "suspected pufferfish poisoning." He must have been a tough old salt who had built up some immunity to bad food, different climates, different insect bites, and different bad alcohol that he had consumed all around the globe to withstand the pufferfish's poison until he died of it at Haslar.

She recalled when Dominique told her about Sobadu and how "He can take the heart of a pufferfish and use it as poison."

"Let me think," she whispered to herself. "I have to be careful. Dr. Foreman said don't jump to conclusions. But this dead sailor's blood looks exactly like my mother's. Maybe she died of pufferfish poisoning like he did."

She let herself feel possible excitement at finding something that would point to the cause of her mother's horrible death. She decided not to look at any more blood samples for the time being until she could show Dr. Foreman what she had found.

Instead, Angeline took the small shavings from the candle and looked at them under the microscope. She didn't think that it would lead to anything, but she did it anyway. The tallow shavings did have some telltale marks, but not enough to add to her theory. Then she looked at the wick cuttings that Dr. Foreman had put on slides. Even under a microscope that produced an image fifty times normal, Angeline couldn't see anything on the wicks that said they had been tampered with. It wasn't as if the juice from the heart of a pufferfish would show up on a candle wick.

When Dr. Foreman checked in on her at the end of the day. Angeline was sitting and moping.

"I can't find anything. I have my doubts that I will ever find anything. But Dr. Foreman, I need you to look at this one slide. The blood from this one sailor slightly resembles my mother's blood sample. Just a little."

Foreman got himself situated at the table with the slides in front of him and looked at both slides for a long time.

"They are similar. I'll hand you that, Angeline," said Dan Foreman. "Very similar. Card says the sailor died of pufferfish poisoning. Did your mom eat pufferfish?"

"Hardly, I remember Mother talking about them in Jamaica, but these waters are too cold for them."

"Right. Now let me see, what should our next step be? First, I will read up on pufferfish tonight. Maybe there's a substitute that can be found in English waters. Can you meet me back here tomorrow afternoon? Perhaps I'll have a better explanation then."

◆ ◆ ◆

The next afternoon, Dr. Foreman entered the lab where Angeline was waiting. She had not processed any more slides. She was hoping upon hope that they had found something.

Foreman started quickly. Angeline could see that he was onto something. "You were right. pufferfish are only in tropical climates where the waters are continually warm. I was reading about them last night. But as I suspected, the toxicology book I was reading said there are substitutes, certain aquatic toads, lizards and the like can be toxic."

"What do we do now?" asked Angeline.

"Well, there is one thing we can do and maybe we could have done it sooner. But suppose that it was pufferfish or toad poisoning. If we could get some, we could burn a bit of it in front of our own noses. Just a little bit mind you; we don't want to suffer as your mother did. Then burn the candle shavings and see if it smells like Dominique's room when you entered it. We'll burn the wick shavings in a similar way. Compare the two. That will prove that this was the type of poison used and that's how she died."

"Will it tell us who did it?"

"Hardly. No. No. Nothing of the sort. You go back to your business. I'll ask Eli Williams to order some pufferfish from LongAcre Supply in London and we should get it in a week's time. They are very prompt in their deliveries and Haslar is a very good customer of theirs. They bring in herbs and poisons and anything you would want in medicine from all over the world.

CHAPTER 15

HASLAR HOSPITAL LAB

Angeline was in the weaving shed with Agnes and Dana, when the message came. It was not a day too soon. Angeline had started to give up hope that she and Dan Foreman would ever find out what killed her mother. Angeline had tried to concentrate on the loom, putting all her physical energy into making the cranky four-poster loom produce cotton sheets faster than it was capable of. She had been pushing the loom bar so hard it was as if she was trying to exorcise a demon from her spirit.

When she read the note that said the pufferfish sample had arrived from LongAcre Supply, Angeline couldn't stop the weaving process fast enough.

"Dana," Angeline called, "take over for me. I have to go to the hospital. I may be there all afternoon, and if I'm not back by five, you and Agnes close up shop for the night."

With that, Angeline, stretched her legs and jogged the half mile to the hospital. After the guards let her in, she made straight for the lab where Dan Foreman was waiting for her.

"Let's set up a controlled burn of a small amount of the poison that LongAcre sent us," said Foreman. "There's enough for a couple of attempts should we need to do more than one test. We should first see what the real poison smells like. It will be up to you to recognize whether or not it was the same smell you noticed when you first discovered Dominique in her room. Listen to me carefully, don't talk yourself into believing this was the smell you experienced. If you're wrong, there could be serious consequences. So be careful, please."

"I understand, Dan," replied Angeline, gearing up mentally for the olfactory challenge in front of her. "What will we do next?"

"After that we'll burn just a bit of the wax, see if the two smells are different or close to the same as the real poison. Then, we'll redo the experiment with the wicks. I have the suspicion that we'll get a stronger smell from the wick shavings so we may want to do that one first. Oh, and I have brought some coffee beans to use as well."

"What are those for?" asked Angeline.

"I learned this in Scotland in school. After smelling the real pufferfish poison, we'll take a strong sniff of the coffee beans to 'clean our noses out' so that we can tell the difference between the second smell and the first without having any residual of the first smell. It works."

"I'll take your word for it."

Dr. Foreman set a small plate on top of a small laboratory tripod and prepared a regular candle to hold under the plate.

"Be careful not to inhale too much of the poison. Remember, we just want an idea of what it smells like. We don't want any of the effect. I'll light the candle and get some heat under the plate. Don't move your nose over the plate until I give the signal. Ready? Here goes."

Dan dipped a small quill tip into the tiny vial of the pufferfish poison and dripped a small amount carefully onto the brass plate. He then lit the candle and gently held it under the tripod. It took a few seconds before either of them could detect any odor. Then when he saw a small whiff of smoke emanate from the tripod, Dan said, "Now Angeline. Inhale. Just a little whiff."

Angeline held her face above the plate on the tripod and took a sniff. As the smoke made its way to her lungs, she felt just a bit woozy with the tiniest bit of an early headache. She backed away from the tripod. Then Foreman took a breath of the pufferfish smoke and then quickly extinguished the flame.

"Well, what did you smell, Angeline? Was it the same smell as was in Dominique's room that morning?"

"Similar. Yes. I would say it was similar," responded Angeline, trying to remember what Dan had said about not trying to force an answer from this experiment. Her wooziness vanished so she didn't even mention it to Foreman.

"Now let's burn some of the wick shavings. I think quite honestly that the candle wax shavings are not going to be as worthwhile as the wicks. We can do that later if we want to."

Dan removed the tin plate with the pufferfish poison and substituted a clean plate. He placed the wick shavings on the new plate. He picked up the small cup of coffee beans that he had taken from the hospital commissary, took a deep breath through his nose and passed it to Angeline so she could do the same.

"Ready? The shavings may take longer to heat up and put out any odor."

"Yes. Go ahead."

Foreman lit the candle and held it under the plate with the wick shavings. It took the better part of a minute for the shavings to heat up and produce a discernable odor.

"Now Angeline, take a whiff of this."

Angeline did as she did before and took a deep breath, this time of the small bit of smoke from the plate. Then Foreman smelled it.

"Smelled enough? I am going to put out the candle. We have so little of the wick shavings that I don't want to waste them."

"That is so close to the pufferfish smell. It is disgusting. I'm convinced," said Angeline.

"So am I. I wasn't in the room when you were, but I will attest to the results I have had smelling both the poison and the wick shavings. If it wasn't the pufferfish poison that was used on the candle wicks it was something darn close," commented the doctor.

"So someone must have entered my mother's bedroom and lit the candles with poisoned wicks without her waking up. How could that have happened? She usually kept the window open at night to get the fresh breeze. But not to wake up? How could that have happened?"

"I don't know, but we do know those candles had poison on the wicks," Foreman said with a note of certainty in his voice.

"Now what do I do?" lamented Angeline.

"That's up to you, Angeline. All you really know is how your mother was killed. You don't know who and you don't know why."

Angeline left Dan Foreman to clean up and put things back in order. Before she left the room, she did something she hadn't planned on doing. She took the vial of unused pufferfish poison that had come from LongAcre Supply and put it into the woven pouch tied around her waist. "If I find out who did this, he can have a long deep draught of his own poison."

Angeline walked back to the weaving shed and a house that by common law would be left to her after her mother's death. There was no one else whom Dominique could give the house to. Angeline took her time with this walk, trying to sort out the information that she and Dan Foreman had discovered through tedious examination of the slides at Haslar and the tests that led to the identification of the poison that had killed her mother.

She thought about her mother and all the times Angeline had been cruel to her. It made her eyes well up with tears. If she could only take back some of the things she had said in anger. If only this... If only that... Her brain was jumbled with a thousand thoughts, not the least of which was how to seek out the person or persons who had poisoned Dominique.

She had her mother's letter which alleged terrible wrongdoing on the part of Sobadu. If Dominique had found a way to tell the Jamaicans in Portsmouth that Sobadu had been a coward during the rebellion and saved his own skin by telling the maroons where to find Tacky, she could have ruined him. The exact words of her letter kept ringing in Angeline's ears.

Sobadu told the maroons where Tacky could be found. They found him, and they killed him. All with Sobadu's help. Sobadu killed my Tacky, killed your father.

If Sobadu knew that Dominique would reveal his dirty secret, he would want her dead, wouldn't he? How could he have come over in the middle of the night and lit those candles? That sounded unlikely but not impossible.

As Angeline walked, she felt deeply alone even though she had friends. What could she expect them to do?

Yes, she had help from Dr. Foreman. Eli had been gracious in his granting of the cotton sheet business. Her helpers, Agnes and Dana, had taken over the weaving while she was examining all those slides under Haslar's microscope. Willie Ferris was a great friend. He always brought a smile to her face. He was always, it seemed, ready to lend a hand. Victor Jerdan ran messages across the bay to Portsmouth when asked. The guards at Haslar had taught her how to defend herself. Who would have thought anyone would take the time to help someone in that way?

Of course, those are the people I have relied on in Gosport. In Portsmouth, I can rely on Michael Harlow and his dad, Jacob. Jacob has helped in the weaving business more than I can repay him for. Michael has taken risks he didn't have to assume. But then why do I feel so alone? Could I ask any one of them to help me get Sobadu? He has to be the one behind this. The letter my mother wrote practically gives chapter and verse to a reason why Sobadu would want her dead. How do I prove it? "Damn," she swore under her breath. *The constabulary won't help. They would just want me to go away. Blacks take care of black justice. Isn't that the message they gave me?*

Angeline had a hundred questions… a hundred thoughts as she walked slowly, stopping every so often to glance back at the hospital. She pulled the pufferfish poison vial from her pouch and looked at it.

If Sobadu was behind her mother's murder, how would she get

him? *I would like to jam this down his throat. How do I convince the police that he did this awful deed? Do I have enough evidence that he did it? Of course, I don't have any proof. What am I thinking? They don't care anyway, what's another dead Jamaican? To them, we're still savages in the jungle. We are chattel that should be yoked to a wagon and worked until we die.*

There was a moment when Angeline's thoughts turned from remorse and speculation to a mission of action that she would commit to. She thought about herself and who she wanted to be. She knew that she was the love child of her mother and Tacky, the African chief who was enslaved in Jamaica and rebelled against the plantation owners. From what her mother had said, Tacky was a tough man who would not succumb to the enslavement he was impressed into.

I will always be Dominique's child. She will always be my mother. And I will keep her memory close to me. But even though I have had many people help me, this search for my mother's killer is up to me and no one else. Maybe Michael can help me, but I don't want to put him in danger. I need to be more like my father Tacky. I have to be as hard-hearted and merciless as he was when he led his rebellion.

◆◆◆

It was after five in the evening when Angeline went to the weaving shed and saw that Agnes and Dana were finished for the day. She would talk to them in the morning but until then she needed to think about what she had to do. Not only for the pursuit of justice for Dominique but also for the business. If he was going to hunt down Sobadu, someone would have to be responsible for the sheet production. She couldn't be in two places at once.

After she saw that the women had left, she went to the house and straight to the kitchen. A dark mood overtook her and she took a brief inventory of the knives. Her mother had fended off an attacker with a spiker cotton carder. She couldn't carry one of those around Portsmouth. She spent the evening as the sun set sharpening the knives. With each stroke with the whetstone, her willingness to kill Sobadu increased. She picked out two that had the right length, sharpness, and feel to them and placed them on the sideboard. She took a third into her bedroom with her. Who knew what the night could bring. She had to sleep. She was dead tired and wanted to be prepared. She also liked to sleep with the window open.

In the morning, Angeline dressed in pants with a wide belt that she could place her knife in. It was commonplace for men to carry knives in an open fashion, but women generally did not. Angeline did not feel like a lady this morning. She greeted Agnes and Dana with money that she kept in the house for payments to her helpers.

"Here's some money that I owe you for taking up the slack when I was at the hospital." She handed each a pound note.

"That's too much," said Agnes, looking at the pound note that represented one month's wages. "You already paid us for this month."

"No, take it. You've earned it. You two have worked twice as hard. I could tell. But there is something else I need your help with."

"What would that be?" asked Dana, ever the quiet one.

"I am going over to Portsmouth and talk with Jacob and Michael Harlow. I have to put together a plan to avenge my mother's death."

"I hope you can find out who did this!" said Agnes with a ferocity Angeline had not heard before.

"So do I," replied Angeline. "I have to do it, there is no one else who will."

"Not the constabulary?" asked Dana.

"No. They don't care about the death of a black woman. They gave me a cold shoulder when Dominique was attacked by Javel. Why should I expect anything different now?"

"What will you do?" asked Agnes.

"I'm not sure. I was hoping that Jacob and Michael would give me advice. I don't know when I'll be back. I just ask the two of you to keep at the weaving the best you can. We must meet our quota every week."

Angeline left them and walked briskly to the ferry and jumped aboard Victor Jerdan's first trip to Portsmouth for the day. The sun

chipped off scrap material. At another dry dock she saw a gang of fifty men pulling ropes using a pulley system to haul a long, heavy mast up to the deck of an older boat that was being refitted.

Without warning, one of the pulley blocks gave way from its mooring. The heavy oaken mast that had been lifted fifteen feet above the ground came crashing down. There was a moment of panic as a shout of, "She's loose!!" came from the bridge of the ship as the men ran away. It was a warning that came much too late.

The mast had crushed two black men who had been pulling on the ropes. There was no saving them. Their death was instant. All Angeline could do from her vantage point was gasp and watch.

The rest of the men who had been pulling on the ropes came to one side of the mast, and with a mighty heave, rolled it a foot or two so they could pull away the bodies of the crushed dead workers. It took a few minutes for the blacks to organize this effort. She saw one black man yelling orders to the others as to where to stand to move the mast in order to extricate the fallen Jamaicans. Not a single white man was in the line to help roll the mast off of the dead men. That ignited something in Angeline, and she walked briskly to the location where the dead men had been placed. The rest of the men had left them and went back to the task at hand.

She bent over and felt a dead man's forehead. She touched another dead man's eyes and closed them in a small silent ceremony. Her spirit was restrained for the moment. No one else but her was near the bodies. They had all been ordered back to work. "God damn them!" she swore to herself. "Do they not have any respect and decency?" Angeline sat there just looking at the dead men.

She watched the workers slowly drift back to where they would attempt to lift the mast again. They couldn't accomplish it right away until the block and pulley system was restrung. She must have stared at the activity for fifteen minutes until she was startled.

Just then, a black man came over to her and quickly asked, "Who are you?"

"Angeline. I'm from Gosport."

"Are you related to either Laverty or Atkins?"

"Those are the dead men's names?"

"Not their African names, but that's what we knew them by."

"And you are?" asked Angeline.

"I'm called Noah. If you're family, you can take the man you're related to. If not, you should leave. The bosses don't like bystanders disrupting the work."

"Disrupting? What do you call a mast falling and killing two men? A bloody inconvenience?" Angeline let the tension come out with a growl.

As Angeline was ready to argue with Noah, two members of the Portsmouth constabulary appeared with a cart and confronted the two of them.

"We understand these two men got killed in an industrial accident. Is that right?" asked one of the policemen.

"Yes," said Noah. "That's right. An industrial accident." He looked straight at Angeline as if to say this happens all the time.

"We'll take the bodies with us. Now be about your business," said one of the constables.

Angeline was dumfounded as to the callousness of the policemen. While they roughly handled the two corpses and carted Laverty and Atkins's remains away in the cart, all Angeline could think was that they would be buried in a potters' field somewhere without kith nor kin to mourn them.

"Officer," Angeline yelled as the cart started away. "Will you be finding out if they have relatives?"

"One of your kind may tell them. We'll have the bodies for the afternoon before they are buried, I'd suspect," one of the policemen yelled back to Angeline.

As Noah walked away from her, Angeline yelled back at him. "Do Laverty or Atkins have family here?"

"No, I don't think so. Nobody knew them well. Maybe Sobadu can tell you. He tends to keep track of us Jamaicans." And with that, Noah was out of earshot.

◆ ◆ ◆

When lunchtime came, Angeline waited around the work site and found Noah sipping his penny beer and gnawing on his bread loaf.

"I want to talk with you alone. Can we sit somewhere else in privacy?" asked Angeline.

Noah was intrigued by this young, bold, black woman, so he agreed and the two separated themselves.

"I only have a half-hour for lunch so it better be quick," said Noah.

"You said Sobadu could tell me who these dead Jamaicans are," stated Angeline not wanting to let Noah know at first that she had met Sobadu.

"That's right. He is a kind of unofficial mayor of the blacks in the Buckland area of Portsmouth, where most of us live. He also acts as policeman, judge, and jury. Stay away from him. He is dangerous," remarked Noah.

Angeline ignored his comment about Sobadu. She already knew how dangerous he was. "How much do you get paid?" she asked impatiently. "I hear it's lower than the white laborers."

"One shilling a day. The whites two shillings a day. The skilled shipwrights four to five shillings a day. We barely make enough to pay the rent. If a man has a family, his wife has to work to survive. Being freed hasn't really brought us freedom. We can leave if we don't like it, but where would we go? Huh, tell me! Where would we go?" Noah clenched his jaw. "I tried asking for more and all I got was a beating... a busted rib and a sore kidney that had me peeing blood for a week."

"They beat you for asking for more money?"

"Not the shipbuilders. Not here. But two men came and found me at night. I don't know who they were. Sobadu didn't do anything when I told him, even though he tells us he'll get justice if we are harmed."

"Sobadu is a fraud and a liar!" hissed Angeline.

"Hoo, listen to the young lady. Such vehemence! How do you know him? You live in Gosport." exclaimed Noah.

"Sobadu got my father killed in Jamaica with his treachery and I think he killed my mother because she knew about it!" Angeline blurted out. She could not bottle up her anger any longer.

"And you want me to care about that? I have to go back to work," said Noah. "Who are you anyway, coming here, causing trouble?"

"I am Jamaican, like you. I am a free woman who runs her own business in Gosport. You should be paid better for this dangerous work."

"I agree with you. All the Jamaicans would agree with you. We don't have physical chains anymore, but we have the chains of low wages. You could call it a law. The iron law of wages."

"Do something about it!" exclaimed Angeline.

"I can't do anything alone. You can't help either," said Noah.

Just then a white overseer named Parkes came close to where the two of them were standing and said in a loud voice, "I heard what you just said. You better shut up about working men's wages, young woman and, Noah, you already know what happens to labor agitators. Get back to work!"

"I am not going to shut up!" Angeline screamed at Parkes, her emotions boiling over. "And you can't make me!"

"We'll see about that," Parkes said. He reached out with his right hand and grabbed Angeline by the back of her coat and pushed her away from the job site. He was a strong man with an equally strong grip and the assault came so fast, Angeline stumbled to her knees and had to make an effort to get back on her feet as she was yanked away. Once on her feet, she scurried her steps to get her body slightly ahead of his, planted her left foot and kicked Parkes in his groin. Her coat was practically ripped from her shoulder, but her action had loosened his grip. It was almost just like the bar fight.

That's what the Fort Moncton guards had taught her. Go for the vulnerable areas. Be swift and sure. Finish your opponent early. The longer the fight lasts the worse your position.

All of that went through Angeline's mind as Parkes let his grip go and gasped for air as he knelt on the gravel. Angeline took a small second step to her right, positioned herself for maximum leverage and delivered a left-footed kick to Parkes' head. Parkes slumped on the ground, blood coming from his busted nose.

Neither Noah nor any other of the Jamaicans who saw what Angeline had done came to her defense or to help Parkes.

Angeline was caught off guard when she was hit in the back of her knees by the rifle butt of a constable. She fell to the ground and was about to be hit again, when she turned onto her back and yelled, "I surrender. I give up. I give up."

She was pulled up from the ground and the constable held her fast as he got ready to haul her away. The constabulary was at least three city blocks away and there were no police carts available in the area since the other two constables had used it for the bodies of Laverty and Atkins.

"Do you want to press charges?" the constable yelled to Parkes.

Parkes had regained his senses, if not his dignity, and rose to spit in Angeline's face and said, "No, but you make sure she doesn't come around here again." He walked up to Angeline, his face right in front of hers, and said, "Or, little missy, you won't be going anywhere but into the bay!"

As she was being dragged away, Angeline yelled out, "Noah, please get Jacob Harlow at his brokerage on Queen Street to come bail me out, please!"

Her voice trailed off as the constable pulled her a little harder to keep up with him. The only thing she heard that lifted her spirits were the cheers and, "Atta Girl!! You got him!" cheers from two or three of the black workers.

◆ ◆ ◆

It wasn't until six in the evening when Jacob and Michael came by the station to pay Angeline's fine for disturbing the peace. Since Parkes didn't press charges, it wasn't an offense that was worthy of a hearing. The only reason for a hearing now would be if Angeline wanted to contest the fine. She didn't. The desk sergeant took their money, gave her a stern warning, and released her to the Harlows.

She was just glad to be out, breathing fresh air and not stuck in a smelly jail overnight. If Parkes had wanted to press charges, the charge might have been elevated to assault. If the police had found the knife Angeline was carrying, the charge might even have been more serious. But as it was, the constabulary didn't have many females in lock up and so they didn't search her at all, which was a relief.

Angeline checked her possessions. She still had the letter, the pufferfish poison, some money, and the knife.

"I imagine you're hungry," said Jacob. "We are as well. I suggest we go to the Hawke Street Pub and have supper."

"As long as I get to pay," said Angeline. "It's no small thing for you to bail me out of jail. The constabulary didn't take my money, so I can pay for our meals."

"That's the spirit, Angeline. You'll have to tell us of your adventures," said Michael. "I have some of my own as well."

The three of them walked to the pub and found a table. There were plenty of people in the pub; some eating, some just drinking the flat British beer.

They ordered their Shepard's pie and beer and waited in silence until their food and drink came. It was hard for Angeline to relax, but she knew she should conserve her energy.

Michael took a long draught of his beer and started. "I found Vincent… you know the guy we talked to at the docks and told us to find Quigley."

"Oh, yes, of course, I remember," said Angeline. The Shepard's pie came, and Angeline gave the bartender the required amount for all three of them. All three dug into their meal and didn't talk while they ate.

Michael finally broke the silence. "I asked Vincent straight away about the wages at the docks and he said that the blacks were paid one shilling a day while the whites were paid twice as much. He said it was hard to survive on that. They needed more. He said Sobadu told them that they should remain calm, that he would take care of their needs."

"Isn't that strange," said Angeline. "Because the man I talked to at the shipyards had been asking for a raise for the blacks… the same wages as the white laborers, and he had been beaten because of it."

Jacob had been eating and listening as the two young folks shared what they had learned. He knew as a businessman that the wage scales were skewed in favor of whites. They had always been. This was a new world to the business owners now. Black men and women were slaves up until two months ago. Now they were paid and wanting more. *It's not going to be a smooth transition*, he thought.

Angeline relayed what had transpired at the shipyards including what Noah had said, the deadly accident, and the fight she had with the white overseer. "Noah doesn't want to see me again. That's for sure. I told him about Sobadu's treachery, but it didn't seem to bother him. Not one little bit. I was discouraged except I heard some of the workers cheer for me as I was being hauled away."

"Oh, sure, you get into a couple of scuffles and kick a foreman bloody and now you got credibility, is that it?" scoffed Michael, who had a well-known reputation as a teen street brawler.

"Well, maybe they'll listen to me," responded Angeline, thinking of a way to get support, a way to weaken Sobadu's hold on the black workers.

"What are you going to do? Make speeches in the middle of the town square? Nobody will listen to you," said Michael, trying to dissuade Angeline from thinking she could change people's minds. It sounded dangerous.

"Yes. Maybe. How do I spread the word that Sobadu is responsible for my father and mother's deaths? Do you think I should just pack up and go back to Gosport, weave sheets and forget about it?" said Angeline angrily.

"Angeline, please keep your voice down," cautioned Jacob as he finished the last of his supper. "We're in a public place. People will hear. I have to leave now. You two talk it out. Thanks for the meal. Oh, and considering the lateness of the hour, accept my invitation to stay at our house tonight."

"Thank you for getting me out of jail," responded Angeline as Jacob pushed his chair back and got ready to leave the pub. Angeline wasn't ready to let the subject drop. "I will take your offer. I can send a note with Victor Jerdan to alert Agnes and Dana as to where I am."

Once Jacob left, Angeline continued. "Michael, you have to understand. That's the point, isn't it? People *need* to hear. Otherwise nothing will change."

"You could get yourself killed. You told me you saw what Sobadu and Slash did to Javel. Right in front of you. If you threaten him, don't think for a minute he wouldn't kill you and get away with it."

"How can I tell people? How do I get them to change their minds about him?"

Michael was worried Angeline's actions would get her killed. "You're not listening to me. You still want to get him? Huh? You want to kill him? Well you will need a rioting crowd to do that for you! Why not put posters up in Buckland where all the blacks are that say 'Hear ye all! Come and hear a woman denounce Sobadu and announce her own suicide!'" Michael said sarcastically. He wanted Angeline to restrain herself from anything as foolish and dangerous as trying to eliminate Sobadu's power.

"Posters?" said Angeline, ignoring the insult. "Will your dad get posters printed for me?"

"Whoa, just a minute. I was kidding. It's a stupid idea. Sobadu will know exactly where you are, and if he or Slash or any one of his thugs hears you, you are a dead woman. Can't you get that through your thick head?"

"Michael, help me, will you?"

Just then Michael saw a poster on a wall in the pub. He got up, went to the poster, and with a small blade, cut its mooring to the wall and brought it over to where he and Angeline were sitting.

"This is interesting," he said. "You want to speak to a crowd of people. Do you care if they are white or black?"

"No. I'll tell anyone of Sobadu's treachery. I have made a solemn oath to avenge my mother."

Michael read the information on the poster. "It says that John Wesley, the traveling preacher, will be in Portsmouth speaking about a mile north from here at some open gardens this coming Sunday. I know that location. Big open space. He'll draw a crowd. It says he'll be speaking on the subject of the British Slave trade. That will certainly draw a crowd. Many will be for him and many will be against him."

"How do I fit in?" asked Angeline.

"You could present yourself to him before he speaks. Ask to say a few words. You can tell him that as a black woman, you'll denounce slavery; the whole institution of it in Britain. They'll let you do that, for sure. Then after you denounce the slave trade, slip in what you want to say about Sobadu. Talk about the type of slavery he holds over the blacks in Buckland. There may be people in the crowd who know him or least know about him. You could get hit by a couple of eggs or tomatoes tossed at you. But what the heck. If you're that nuts…"

"Doesn't everyone agree with John Wesley?" asked Angeline naively.

"Are you kidding? How do you think London, Bristol, Manchester, Liverpool, Portsmouth, and other English cities got to be so wealthy? They grew rich on the backs of the slave trade for two hundred years. The people whose livelihoods depend on it don't want it to change. You don't think they're going to take this recent Mansfield decision lying down, do you? The newspapers have reported that there have been street riots all over the country since the end of June. Why it hasn't happened here in Portsmouth is a mystery."

"I'm going to Wesley's speech," said a determined Angeline. "I'm going to ask him if I can speak to the crowd."

"I'll be in the back," replied Michael. "Watch out for the rotten eggs."

CHAPTER 17

THE GARDENS

A crowd of almost three hundred people made their way to the gardens to hear John Wesley speak. His reputation preceded him and many of the people who came were interested in hearing a speech about the evils of slavery. Wesley had been traveling throughout England for twenty years preaching his "Methodism" attracting many to his cause. His passion was to rid England of the scourge of slavery.

Wesley's cause drew people to him but also attracted rabid detractors who in different parts of the country had attacked him and his small group and tried to imprison him. It was a time when an anti-slavery sermon could not be preached without considerable personal risk to the preacher.

On this particular Sunday afternoon, Wesley's crowd consisted of churchgoers of many denominations, but mostly Anglicans, some of whom were anti-slavery, some still pro-slavery. There were those who genuinely wanted to hear what he had to say but there were also those with a crate of tomatoes to fling. Speech making in the open-air forums was often hazardous. Only a few people from the Portsmouth Jamaican population showed up. They stayed well back from the main crowd.

Angeline ignored all of Michael's suggestions. She had reached Wesley before he started talking and boldly asked for the stage after he spoke. It was a strange request but when Angeline told him that she was once a slave and would speak on its evils, Wesley was inclined to let her speak. Because of her passion and her anger simmering below the surface, he seemed to think Angeline would add to the strength of his message.

In his hour-long speech, Wesley vilified the English slave trade with passion. It was his zeal for ending slavery that drew the audiences to his words, including Angeline. She stood close to the makeshift stage which was roughly constructed on the bed of a wagon high enough so the crowd could see and hear him. She listened intently and was taken in by the truth she heard in his words.

"Slavery is said to arise from captivity in war... slavery may begin, by one man's selling to another. And it is true, a man may sell himself to work for another: but he cannot sell himself to be a slave... Thirdly, that men may be born slaves, by being the children of slaves.

"So that whatever he or the African does in this matter is all your act and deed. And is your conscience quite reconciled to this? Does it never reproach you at all? Has gold entirely blinded your eyes, and stupefied your heart? Can you see, can you feel, no harm therein? Is it doing as you would be done to? Make the case your own. 'Master,' said a slave at Liverpool to the merchant who owned him 'what, if some of my countrymen were to come here, and take away my mistress, and Master Tommy, and Master Billy, and carry them into our country, and make them slaves, how would you like it?' His answer was worthy of a man: 'I will never buy a slave more while I live.'

"Oh let his resolution be yours! Have no more any part in this detestable business. Instantly leave it to those unfeeling wretches who laugh at human nature and compassion! Be you a man, not a wolf, a devourer of the human species! Be merciful, that you may obtain mercy!

"Give liberty to whom liberty is due, that is, to every child of man, to every partaker of human nature. Let none serve you but by his own act and deed, by his own voluntary action. Away with all whips, all chains, all compulsion. Be gentle toward all men; and see that you invariably do with everyone as you would he should do unto you."

When he ended his impassioned speech, he introduced Angeline as an ex-slave from Jamaica. As she mounted the stage, excitement coursed through her entire body. She had never spoken to a crowd before. She had exorcised her anger more than a few times but only one-on-one or with two or perhaps three people. Never with three hundred. She knew she had to "find her voice" quickly or people would walk away thinking that the main speaker, Wesley, was done and there would be no more.

When she looked out over the crowd, she thought hard about what she wanted to say. She said a small prayer to her mother to help her find her killer. That small moment of prayer emboldened her and gave her the power in her voice that she needed. She would speak as loudly as she could even to the point of yelling.

"I was a slave!" Angeline boomed. "You people in this crowd who are white have never known what it means to be a slave. What it means never to have an independent thought. What it means to have your bread and butter and sometimes your life itself determined by the whim of another. But I can tell you. My mother and I were slaves in Jamaica. We were household servants lucky not to work in the sugar cane fields under the whip, neck iron, or yoke of a vicious overseer. We were bought by a Scottish couple who raised me in the teachings of the Christian bible. Yes. You heard me. The bible. And I can quote passages just like you. From Deuteronomy which you all know: *Rejoice, O ye nations, with his people: for he will avenge the blood of his servants, and will render vengeance to his adversaries, and will be merciful unto his land, and to his people. The righteous shall rejoice when he seeth the vengeance: he shall wash his feet in the blood of the wicked.*"

The crowd up front murmured among themselves, loud enough

so Angeline could hear. "The black woman knows the bible. How amazing!"

It emboldened Angeline even further. She continued her speech. "Who are the wicked? Is it you? Is it you? Have you participated willingly or unwillingly in the slavery of others? As Reverend Wesley has suggested, if you drink rum or use sugar made from sugar cane, you have fostered slavery. Look to your souls. Boycott these things! Don't buy them!

"Blacks have been freed in England by the Mansfield decision for only two months. But the slave trade continues, doesn't it? There are slaves in Jamaica yet and in the colonies, are there not? What makes England so special? In Jamaica my mother and I were runaways. We could have been killed for that. Our killers would never have to face justice until they met the Almighty! We were lucky when we were caught and sold to the Scottish couple. They treated us well.

"My mother and I were sold again to Dr. Duncan at Haslar Hospital across the bay in Gosport and sold again to Dr. Jim Hawkins who gave us our papers declaring us free. Yes. Totally free. Just like you. Now, I am an independent businesswoman and I work hard, as hard as any of you. I am no different than you except for one thing. My mother has been murdered! Yes, murdered in her own bed. I have good evidence that Sobadu has done this. Those of you from Portsmouth know of Sobadu. Sobadu of Buckland! This is the same Sobadu who gives liquor and drugs to free Jamaicans. He wants to keep them in another form of slavery; slavery to him and the drugs he gives them. This man killed my mother!

"There is another form of slavery that still exists in Portsmouth. The Jamaicans are not paid what they are worth. They are not paid what white people are paid to do the same work. They still have chains. They still cannot afford basic necessities of life. They are chained by the iron law of slave wages."

Just then, someone in the crowd threw a tomato at Angeline and hit her in the shoulder. That person yelled, "They get what they deserve. They get what they deserve. Which isn't much!" A few people around the tomato thrower laughed.

Angeline yelled back at her heckler. "You want to be paid a righteous wage, don't you? They do too!"

Another tomato came flying onto Angeline. This one hit her in the leg.

"Your tomatoes will not turn me away!" Angeline screamed. "Meet me face to face and I'll shove your tomatoes in your face."

Without another word from Angeline, one of Reverend Wesley's followers came up on the wagon bed and physically pulled Angeline down off the stage. She resisted, and barely missed getting hit with another tomato. While being pulled off the stage, she looked back to catch a glimpse of her heckler so she could chase him down and beat him if she could. She was being dragged so roughly that she fell. Her knees collapsed and she fell to the ground as an egg was thrown and missed the two of them.

"Don't yell back at them. It only makes them angrier," the man said.

"I will defend myself!" shouted Angeline, picking herself up.

The clamor from a few more dissenters filled the air with hateful talk, and a few black slurs were tossed Angeline's way. "Black bastard child, I'll bet you are," the voice yelled.

"Get back home," another shouted.

"You can't tell us what to think. Go back to Jamaica, make us some rum!" yelled another.

For fear that the crowd would get violent, Wesley's companions swept Angeline to the back of the wagon, and physically led her down a path that went away from the crowd. Angeline resisted them and wanted to go back and confront the men who had either hurled insults or threw the tomatoes and eggs.

Michael was way in the back, but he heard Angeline's speech and heard the insults thrown at her. He also saw the rotten projectiles tossed at her. He left his position in the rear and ran around the crowd to join up with her.

As he started running to help Angeline, he noticed a couple of small groups of Jamaicans who had kept to themselves at the rear of the crowd. He spotted one man he thought he knew. It was the same black man who had followed him, his dad, Dominique, and Angeline after Javel's execution. He wondered why that man was there.

◆ ◆ ◆

Delroy was amazed by what he had heard at the Wesley rally. He didn't know exactly what to make of it. His mind was awhirl with contradicting thoughts. He knew that the blacks were free, but he didn't know slavery was still happening. Although his mind told him he was free, his soul knew he was a lowly paid slave to Sobadu.

The black woman's words haunted him. Did Sobadu kill the woman's mother? Was he knowingly making the Jamaicans slaves to him? Delroy had never questioned the power of Sobadu before, and it made him very uneasy. He could keep it to himself and let Sobadu find out on his own. Or Delroy could make himself more indispensable and tell the Obeah man what he had heard.

He made his decision reluctantly and went to find Sobadu to tell him what he had heard. He had a job, although he was not paid well for the messages he delivered for Sobadu. He reluctantly felt that he had a place, an existence that meant something to him and allowed him to survive and not do manual labor at the docks.

Delroy left his small group of fellow Jamaicans who had listened to the speeches and made his way down to Buckland.

Delroy had fulfilled his master's wishes by reporting things to him that he had heard that could be important to him. He detested the way he was treated by Sobadu and Slash, but he thought he needed to tell him what he had heard even if it meant incurring his wrath.

Two of Sobadu's henchmen who guarded the door refused to let Delroy get by to his own room until one of them went upstairs and contacted Slash who then received permission from Sobadu to let Delroy come up. The fact that it was Delroy's small flat made no difference to Sobadu. He took what he wanted from any of the Jamaicans. He said they owed him his tribute.

Delroy went into his room to find Slash and Sobadu preparing drugs for the Sunday night "ritual" at the warehouse. The salvia, jimsonweed, and other hallucinogenic herbs were being collected and separated as needed to be infused with the rum that would be provided.

"I went to hear the anti-slavery speech at the gardens," said Delroy. "Some guy named Wesley or Welsey—I can't remember—spoke for an hour."

"And you're telling me this because?" questioned Sobadu, never lifting his eyes from the table at which he was separating herbs for the evening's ritual. "Why should I care? He speaks all over England about ending slavery, so what?" barked Sobadu.

"When he was done, a black woman got up on the stage and… talked about her and her mother in Jamaica and in England."

"Get to the point. I am very busy," demanded Sobadu.

Delroy spoke the next sentence with trepidation. He stuttered, hemmed and hawed until Sobadu demanded he spit out whatever he was going to say.

"She said that you keep the Jamaicans here in chains by giving them drugs. She said that her mother died in her own bed. That you murdered her mother and that you—"

"What did you say, you sniveling little rat?" bellowed Sobadu. "Did I hear you right? Did you say she spoke to a crowd of people and said I killed her mother? Did she use my name?!"

Delroy couldn't speak, he was shaking so violently. After a small nod from Sobadu, Slash drew his machete and put it hard and sharp against Delroy's throat. Delroy thought that he would be killed on the spot for bringing bad news.

"Is this the truth?" yelled Sobadu, clearly in a rage. "If you are making this up, Slash will kill you now, and the bay will have your body by sunset!"

"I swear on my mother's grave. That's what I heard," said Delroy. "Yes, she used your name."

"Did she say anything else?" asked Sobadu, staring into Delroy's face from four inches away.

"She said something about Jamaicans getting paid less than whites for the same work, but I was in the back and didn't hear everything clearly," said Delroy, wanting to appease the big man so Sobadu would move away from him.

Sobadu motioned to Slash and he removed his machete from Delroy's face. "What was the woman's name?" demanded Sobadu.

"Whose name?" asked Delroy, shaking and relieved that the machete was no longer at his throat. He put a hand to his throat and pulling it away noticed a small amount of blood.

"The woman who spoke, you idiot, the woman who spoke."

"She was introduced as Angeline."

"Angeline. Was she Jamaican? Did she say her mother's name?"

"No, not her mother's name. And she said she was Jamaican," said Delroy, hoping he could get permission to leave the room.

"Get out of here. I have to think. All of you, get out of here!" yelled Sobadu with an angry, worried look on his face.

Delroy took a last look at what he thought was once his room and went down the stairs. He brushed past the two henchmen who guarded the door and practically stumbled down the street. He felt his throat again and wondered if the next time Slash threatened him, it would mean his death.

Delroy slumped in an alley and leaned against a wall of crates. He had to shoo away a couple of rats before he could sit down and think.

If he'd kill me for just bringing him news, what would he do if he had a real cause. I don't want Slash to kill me on some whim of his. I would like to end his miserable life. Then maybe mister big Obeah man might not feel so invulnerable and almighty. I need a knife. No. Slash is too good in a knife fight. I need a gun and I need one now.

Delroy got up from his slouched position and went back into the streets.

I don't have the money to buy a pistol. They're expensive. I know, I'll steal Quigley's gun. I know he has one. I've been in his shop getting drugs to take to Sobadu and he's pulled it on me, warning me against taking anything from his dirty little shop. I'll take that gun, it'll serve him right.

◆ ◆ ◆

When Michael caught up to Angeline, she was one hundred feet from the back of the wagon where she had spoken a few minutes earlier. She was slightly frightened by the heckling and vegetable throwing, but angry just the same. It took more than a few moments for Wesley's men to calm her down. They praised her for having the courage to speak in front of the large crowd. They told her she was braver than many, many others. It was comforting to hear, but those words didn't make her comfortable or serene. Her adrenaline from the excitement elevated her entire being. She was elated with overcoming the challenge of public speaking. She was emboldened by what she thought was a positive response from the crowd. She may have just imagined their acceptance of her. It could have been a mere novelty seeing a black woman not only making a speech but quoting the bible at them.

When Michael caught up to her, Angeline asked him if he thought the audience took note of what she had said.

"Yes, Angeline, that bible quote got everyone to take notice, that's for sure. Some of them thought you were going to 'seek your vengeance upon them and wash your feet in their blood,'" said Michael.

"Made my point, do you think?" said Angeline.

"Oh, definitely made your point. Did you actually call them wicked?"

"Well, they buy the rum and the sugar from Jamaica, don't they?"

"Sure, doesn't everybody?"

"There you have it, Michael. There you have it. England gets drunk on the backs of slaves. Makes for quite a headline in the newspaper, don't you think?"

"You gonna write the story?"

"No, but you could. Better yet, get the newspaper people to write it. You know anybody?" Angeline's excitement was growing. Rather than be defeated by the tomato tossing, she was energized and she was looking for a way to spread the news. She had just stood up on a wagon and accused a powerful man of murder.

For a moment, Michael thought she was crazy, and might have had a death wish so she could join her mother in paradise. But his rational mind discounted those ideas. No, Angeline didn't seem to feel that way. She wanted Sobadu to die, and she needed his help.

"The Morning Post might print something," said Michael. "They're always looking for some gossip, some scandal, or something controversial that will sell newspapers."

"That's something you could do in the morning. You could see if anyone from the Post was there and if they're willing to jump into the fray. They could print a story about the low wages for the Jamaicans."

"That would be treading on some toes, Angeline. You ask too much, too soon," warned Michael. She had announced her hatred of Sobadu, a powerful man, and now she wanted to take on the entire power structure with this idea. She would be up against the Admiralty, shipbuilders, and merchants. That would be crazy. She needed them more than they needed her to stir the anger of the workers.

"Did my mentioning the wage issue get a response from the crowd?" asked Angeline.

"You saw the response it got," said Michael. "You got peppered with tomatoes and eggs. And that was from white people. There weren't many Jamaicans there. I saw just a few in the back. It was mostly white folks, from the city and the outlying areas."

"I have to spread the word about Sobadu's treachery," spoke Angeline hurriedly.

"Slow down, will you? Just slow down. You have to think this through."

"That's your problem Michael. You want to be logical. The Jamaicans aren't going to want logic. They will want action. That's the difference. You are not going to win them with newspaper articles. That's for the white people who can read. The Jamaicans have been ill-educated so they can be controlled. Education for them and their children has been almost non-existent... on purpose."

Michael interrupted her rant. "Education doesn't happen overnight. It takes years."

"I don't have years. We can get my message to the whites and we can get the message in another form to the blacks. Can I stay at your house tonight? I have a plan for early tomorrow and then, I promise I'll go back to Gosport for a couple of days and work the loom. I want to 'stir the pot' some more."

Angeline pulled her mother's final letter from her pocket and gave it to Michael. "You've read this letter, haven't you? You know how damning it is?"

"Yes," said Michael.

"Take it to the Morning Post, get them to write about what Wesley said about banning sugar and rum, slip this into the article as well. That will alert the white people who read it of Sobadu's treachery."

"What are you going to do?"

"Make the same speech tomorrow morning that I made today."

"Where?" asked Michael. It was no use trying to dissuade Angeline. She was racing to judgment. Michael just hoped it wasn't her last judgment.

"To the black workers at the shipyards, that's where. I'll blend a little religion with a call to justice. I heard what Wesley did in his speech. He used the bible to establish a sense of righteousness. Then he called for justice for the black man; justice for the slave. That's what I'll do. They can't arrest me for preaching the gospel, can they?"

"You're not a minister. Who appointed you?" questioned Michael sharply.

"Doesn't matter. Not to the Jamaicans. They let Sobadu feed them mystic Obeah rubbish on Sunday nights. They can listen to the Christian bible spoken to them."

Michael was being bowled over with Angeline's persistence. "All right, say you can get an audience and the shipbuilders don't throw you in jail. Then what?"

"Then I'll head straight for the dock and get a ferry ride home. Let the pot boil for a day or two. See what happens. You said I need help with this crusade. Well, I have to get the Jamaicans to go against Sobadu and they need to hear this story."

"What if you get arrested? What if you get beaten up? I can't always be there. I have to work too. My dad has been very patient with you; very helpful I would say. We have supported you, haven't we?"

"Do you want to see my mother avenged?"

"Yes, of course."

"Then help me. Please."

"All right. All right," conceded Michael. "I'll give the information to the Morning Post."

"I'll need that letter returned. Don't let them keep it. It's a memory of my mother that I want to hold onto."

"All right, I'll show it to them, but no promises. It's their paper after all," replied Michael.

"I'll speak to the blacks at the shipyards, tomorrow morning, bright and early as they're headed for work," said Angeline excitedly. "Then I'll scamper. I promise. For now, I have to get a message over to the docks so Jerdan can tell Agnes and Dana what I'm up to. I'll meet you at your house."

CHAPTER 18

PORTSMOUTH: THE SHIPYARDS

In the Harlow's spare bedroom, that night before she fell asleep, Angeline looked at the bible beside her and paged through it looking for the words that would elevate her spirit in front of a crowd. She wanted the same courage that buoyed her spirits when she spoke at the gardens after Wesley's speech the previous afternoon.

Angeline left Jacob Harlow's house at dawn and quickly made her way to the docks. As she walked, she took a moment to think about what Michael had said yesterday. He was willing to help her avenge the death of her mother. He agreed that Sobadu had killed her mother or had her killed. But it was worrisome that she was asking him to take risks to help her. She had left a note for him at the house, asking him to meet her at the Hawke Street Pub at lunchtime. Although she was going back on her promise to go home, she wanted to hear if the Morning Post would print her story. And she still fretted about her relationship with Michael.

If I ask too much, he'll balk and I won't even have him as a friend, thought Angeline. *He likes the adventure of it all; the street fight is a challenge to him. But my mother was killed, not his. I am the one who wants to see Sobadu dead.*

Angeline arrived at the shipyards before any of the workers

ambled in. She got to a spot where she thought many would pass by and found an empty, heavy hogshead to stand on. She had to speak quickly when she had her chance. The last time she was at the shipyards just talking with Noah, she got into a scuffle with a foreman, knocked with a rifle butt, and got hauled off to the constabulary. She didn't have any backup this time. Michael wasn't there. Jacob wasn't there to bring his status should there be any argument with authorities. No one would help her if she was accosted. This made her nervous and wary, yet strong at the same time. She reached around her back and felt the long blade that she had hidden in her belt and under her jacket.

She thought about her mother cold in the earth at Haslar Hospital unable to take a breath of the ocean breeze that blew into Portsmouth harbor. She allowed the sadness to overcome her. But she was different from other people who might let the grief soften them. She gathered strength and resolve from it. She looked down at the crystal around her neck, remembering that it was a gift from her mother that she would always have close to her. Her right hand, then her left caressed the crystal as she asked for strength.

Her plan was to speak as much as she could, as quickly as she could, to as many as she could, jump down off the hogshead cask, and run down to the docks where she would do the same in front of a different audience. She knew that one day of preaching wouldn't do it. She needed to do this over several days. But did she have the time?

Angeline stood on the hogshead with the bible in her hand. She had it opened to the passage she wanted. When the first eight or nine black men from Buckland walked in front of her, she read the eight beatitudes from Jesus's sermon on the mount. She held the bible in her left hand and used her right arm to gesticulate into the air as if she was an open-air preacher convincing the wayward to repent. She read loudly but slowly for emphasis, fully intending to repeat herself for each group that went by. She wanted attention.

"Listen to me, your hardships will be rewarded. Listen to what

Jesus said in His sermon on the mount in front of thousands of people:"

> Blessed are the poor in spirit: for theirs is the kingdom of heaven.
> Blessed are the meek: for they shall possess the earth.
> Blessed are you who mourn: for you shall be comforted.
> Blessed are you who hunger and thirst for justice: for you shall be satisfied.
> Blessed are the merciful: for you shall obtain mercy.
> Blessed are the clean of heart: for you shall see God.
> Blessed are the peacemakers: for you shall be called the children of God.
> Blessed are they that suffer persecution for justice's sake, for yours is the kingdom of heaven.

Of those who passed by her, a couple of them stopped to listen. Some kept walking and didn't pay any attention. She was a bit of a rarity, a preacher on a Monday morning. As she was reading these beatitudes slowly, a few more men came and stopped. There were ten or so who slowly walked by trying to grasp what the woman standing on the hogshead was saying.

"Do you suffer persecution for justice sake?" Angeline yelled. "Of course you do. You work for low wages. Lower than the white man's. Well, don't you? Yours will be the kingdom of heaven.

"Do you hunger and thirst for justice? Yes. You do the dirty work, the hard work, the exhausting work. Well, the bible sermon says you will be satisfied. Rise up against the oppression. You are not slaves any longer. Assert the rights that are yours!"

Noah and two others came close where Angeline was speaking.

Noah had been severely beaten for agitating for higher pay, so he immediately feared for Angeline's safety. One of Noah's friends said to him and the other man, "I recognize her, don't you, she's the one who drove Parkes to the ground. She's a fighter. Let's see what happens."

"Angeline, come down from there!" Noah shouted. "You're not safe there."

"Noah?" said Angeline looking down from her unsteady perch. "I am safe. I'm preaching the gospel. How can that be wrong?" replied Angeline defiantly.

"In its time and in its place, Angeline, you can preach the Christian bible. But you cannot yell to workers about their rights. We have none. You cannot tell us to rise against oppression. You will be beaten, even killed. Get down from there!"

"No. Not unless someone takes me from here."

Noah turned around and saw two white overseers walking quickly towards them. They were accompanied by a member of the constabulary who was armed with a musket. Noah and his two companions walked away, but looked back at what they knew was going to be an ugly scene.

It was Parkes again. "Get down from there or we'll pull you down!" Parkes barked.

"I am preaching the Christian gospel to people walking to work. Why would that be a crime? I am within my rights."

The constable stepped forward and spoke to Parkes. "She's right. This is public ground she's on. It's not shipyard property, not technically."

Parkes turned to the constable and said, "She's disturbing the peaceful work of the shipyards. Arrest her."

"I can't arrest her if she's on public ground," said the constable.

"Well then the least you can do is move her away from my workers. She's a troublemaker!"

"That's good enough for me. All right, young lady, off the barrel! You're coming with me!"

Angeline stood there defiantly and yelled as loud as she could to the crowd that was walking to work. "You have nothing to lose but your chains. Sobadu killed my mother. Sobadu killed my mother! Sobadu killed my mother!"

At that outburst, Parkes kicked the barrel and Angeline came crashing to the ground. She rose quickly, threw down the bible, and took a defensive posture ready to protect herself.

The constable took his rifle and braced it across his chest, got between the two of them, turned toward Parkes, and pushed him back a couple of feet. When Parkes resisted, the constable pushed him again. "One more step, Parkes, and you'll be the one going to jail," the constable said.

Parkes stopped, turned around, and started walking in the direction of the shipyards. But before he was out of earshot, he yelled at Angeline, "You come back here again and there won't be anyone to protect you. Consider yourself warned."

And with that, he kept walking until he was out of sight. With Parkes and Noah and his companions gone, all that was left on the scene was the constable and Angeline. She dusted herself off and was trying to place the hogshead in an upright position when the constable stopped her.

"Don't put that barrel back. You're not getting up on it again. You made your point. Parkes made his. Now you move along. Preach your sermon somewhere else. I mean it."

He took a step towards Angeline. She got the message and did not want to feel the sting of the rifle butt again. She picked up her bible and strode away from the shipyards and in the direction of the docks.

When she got to the docks, which were but a quarter mile or so from the shipyards, she saw many men moving cargo off the ships that had come in from the colonies. The cotton bales were everywhere, along with the tobacco, deerskins, lumber, and a myriad assortment of other goods from the Americas and the Caribbean.

She didn't have so much of a plan as it was a path that she was on and had to take. *This is something that is inside my spirit, I cannot run away from this. I cannot go back to Gosport and weave cotton. I have to do this.*

Angeline found a place that she thought was on a public street. There were dozens of people walking by at this time of the morning. Dock workers were moving goods to and from warehouses. Merchants were hustling to a meeting or directing where the goods they purchased should be stored. There was general congestion among people, horses, and the carts they hauled. There was so much traffic that they could easily bump into one another. She could see the cotton exchange in the distance where Jacob Harlow would soon be busy buying and selling cotton.

She had to make a stand here. There were plenty of Jamaicans moving merchandise on carts, off of ships, up and down the dock. This was a good place to get her message out. She found an empty crate on the dock and moved it to where some people could see her. This was the third time that she would speak in public. It was getting easier.

She started with the sermon on the mount again. She had to be loud to be heard among the cacophony of the noise on the docks. Her voice was getting more confident and much louder.

Blessed are the poor in spirit.

Blessed are the meek: for they shall possess the earth.

Blessed are you who mourn: for you shall be comforted.

Blessed are you who hunger and thirst for justice: for you shall be satisfied.

She yelled to the open air for any ears that wanted to hear. "You want justice, don't you? Release your chains of bondage! You need to be paid as much as the white laborers! Hear me, my fellow black laborers. You are slaves no longer. You are freemen. Free to withhold your labor if you are not paid what you are worth. You must unite. You must work together to get what you want. You shall have to work for justice. I want justice too. Sobadu killed my mother! Sobadu killed my mother! Sobadu killed my mother!

A black man came right up to her and said, "What are you doing? You can't talk like this. You'll be killed."

"Vincent? Is it you? We spoke days ago. You told us to find Quigley, remember?"

Vincent tried to dodge knowing this woman standing on a crate in the morning sun yelling into the air. "I don't remember anything of the sort. All I know is that you will be hurt if you talk like this."

"You are not a slave any longer, Vincent. Don't be treated like one. Stand up for your rights!"

"You're a fancy one to talk. You'd better get down from there, or there will be trouble."

"Help me, Vincent. Talk to your friends on the docks. Convince them to ask for the same wages that the white laborers get. If you don't act like a free man, you'll never be one. You'll live in the slums of Buckland your entire life."

◆ ◆ ◆

It was a bizarre scene for two hours. Since she was on a public street, the constables walked by and stared at her but never made her move, unlike the police at the shipyards. Angeline talked, and recited bible quotes when she couldn't think of what to say. She never once restrained herself from blaming Sobadu for her mother's death. She was a town crier on a dock in Portsmouth and she never really knew if anyone listened to her.

But one person did. Delroy had stumbled out of his rough hallway tenement and walked to the docks where he saw Angeline standing on a crate spouting from a bible and yelling for justice. He stood aside in an adjacent alley and watched and listened. What he heard might be valuable.

At the end of roughly two hours, she got down from her makeshift pulpit and walked with a feeling of dejection. She had received two or three catcalls, two or three genuinely vulgar racist comments, a couple of "You tell 'ems" and the attention of a few people who stopped and listened for a moment or two.

She kept trying to tell herself that in order to get support from the black workers, and maybe from some of the white community, she may have to do this again and again and again to make any impact at all.

She strode toward the Hawke Street Pub where she had arranged to meet Michael. On the way, she saw a paperboy on the corner selling the Morning Post. Although it was about noon, the paper had printed something and had its paperboys selling it on the street. She was astonished when she gave the boy a penny from her pocket and read the headline: "England Drinks on Backs of Slaves." It was only a one sheet newspaper with printing on one side.

Angeline read the article which detailed Wesley's speech from the day before. Michael couldn't possibly have reached them in time for them to set type and print this. But there it was. They must have had a writer take notes on Sunday and put something together for this morning's printing. But what got her excited was the end of the story: "Gosport Woman says Mother Was Murdered." The headline only received one small paragraph, but it had her name, her mother's name, and an excerpt from her mother's note. There was Sobadu's name, with language that vaguely asserted that he had been suspected in a crime. They left out the backstory about what had happened in Jamaica. She was surprised so she read it again and then a third time. There it was: a printed allegation.

Someone important will read this. Someone will take action and put Sobadu in jail, she thought.

She saw Michael in the corner of the tavern and went over to him, newspaper in hand.

"How did you get them to print this?"

"Aren't I the gentle persuader?" said Michael.

"No you're not," answered Angeline. "But tell me how you did it, so if I need to, I know what strings to pull to get another story printed."

Michael handed over Dominique's letter that Angeline had given him. It had helped convince the newspaper editor that the allegations had substance.

"I have to admit it. My dad knows the owner of the paper. That got me the interview with them when they first opened this morning. The story alone would have got it printed. As I said earlier, they love scandal and corruption stories. They think they can hold city government accountable for their behavior. But that has about as much chance to succeed as fish swimming upstream."

As the two of them ordered their noontime bowl of fish stew and a pint of beer, Mayor Cady and Phil Varlo came into the pub and sat in the booth behind them. When Michael heard the mayor's and the alderman's names mentioned, Michael motioned for Angeline to be quiet. He raised a silent finger up to his mouth as he slid down in his seat out of sight and motioned for Angeline to do the same.

"Did you see the 'Morning Post' this morning, Mister Mayor?" asked Varlo pointedly.

"Keep your voice down, Varlo," said Cady. "We shouldn't even be meeting here. And yes, I read it. That Wesley knows how to stir up a hornet's nest of trouble. I expect the Shipbuilders and the Admiralty will be on my neck this afternoon."

"That's not the part I was referring to. Some woman spoke to the crowd and named Sobadu as the killer of her mother. Do you know anything about that?"

"No and we shouldn't even be talking about him here," commented Cady in as low a voice as he could muster.

"All right, but this should interest you. One of my people told me this morning that she also told the crowd that the Jamaicans are not paid what they're worth. She said they're not paid what white people are paid for the same work."

"I thought you 'paid a visit' to the labor agitator. What was his name?" demanded Cady.

"His name is Noah, and yes," replied Varlo, "we got our point across. Parkes at the shipyard told me that Noah has shut his mouth out higher wages. This woman is different. She doesn't work at the yards or on the docks."

"A woman you say? There will always be complainers," commented Cady trying to pass the story off as irrelevant.

"The difference is she is complaining in public," stated Varlo. "She's making speeches in public in front of hundreds of people. Followers of Wesley and churchgoing anti-abolitionists like him who want to stop the slave trade."

"Do you know who she is? She needs to shut up about this. Is she white or black?" questioned Cady, his mind racing for a solution. He didn't have to put down every labor agitator, but one who was speaking in public was another kettle of Atlantic cod altogether.

Varlo replied, "She's a black woman. In her speech she said she was a Jamaican who had been given her freedom by a doctor at Haslar Hospital."

As a cowardly politician Cady had an easy, expedient solution. "If she's black, we can get Sobadu to shut her up."

"He'll want more money," responded Varlo.

"Will you shut up about money, Varlo. Damn it! Where do you think we are?" Varlo never knew how to keep sensitive issues quiet. He was always too vocal and too loose-lipped.

Varlo took a long draught from his beer glass. "I know exactly where we are. And we already pay Sobadu plenty to keep the Jamaicans from demanding more money. We shouldn't have to pay him anything more."

"You know, of course, that as public officials, we're paid to make sure that happens. Tell you what, Varlo. Tell your contacts at the shipbuilders to lay off a crew of the black laborers. Tell them there's a slowdown in the works."

"Even if it's not true?" questioned Varlo.

"When does that matter?" said Cady. "This will soften the resolve of the ones left working. Threat of unemployment will get their attention."

"And what about Sobadu?"

"He's my concern, not yours," said Cady trying to shut down the conversation. "I'm leaving. As far as we're concerned, I was never here and never heard what you said. I'll deny it as long as I live." He rose quickly and left. He glanced around sideways at people who were in the vicinity but saw no one that he considered to be a threat.

What he didn't know was that Michael and Angeline were hiding out of sight on the floor next to the booth where Cady and Varlo had been. They had heard everything.

When they thought Varlo and Cady were completely out of the tavern, they popped their heads up and looked at each other.

"Did you hear what I heard?" asked Angeline, wanting to get Michael to confirm the awful truth of government corruption.

"I did. The mayor and a councilman are paying Sobadu to keep the Jamaicans' wages down."

"Why would they do that?" asked Angeline naively.

"Simple, really simple. Keeping their wages down below the whites does two things. It makes the shipyards and merchants at the docks richer and keeps a wedge between the black workers and the whites doing the same job. If you think someone will work for less, you're more apt to keep working harder. It's a simple, yet time tested strategy of the streets."

"Which you know so well. We need to get out of here and talk about what we're going to do," said Angeline.

"Was that 'we?'" said Michael with a false sense of incredulity.

"Maybe we… maybe just me," replied Angeline as the two of them scurried out of the tavern.

CHAPTER 19

PORTSMOUTH DOCKS

Angeline's energy was contagious. Michael wanted to help her, but his dad had asked him to work and he acceded to the request. There was warehouse organization to accomplish for the bales of cotton going into and out of the warehouse. Each bale's weight needed to be verified and shipping bills needed to be checked before the cotton could be sent to the purchasers. Jacob did the buying and selling, and Michael managed the warehouse work. All the numbers in the office that Jacob put together had to balance with what was received and shipped. It could get very busy with the quantity of cotton coming into England from the colonies. Michael could afford to let some of the warehouse management be delegated to a trusted foreman for a few hours a day, but he couldn't do it for an extended period of time.

Michael was torn between doing his job, helping his dad's business succeed, and helping Angeline, who seemed at the same time to be a driven spirit and a lost cause, preaching the bible and yelling to the heavens about the death of her mother. It would get her killed, Michael just knew it. He had been on the streets of Portsmouth too long not to have seen what people in power were willing to do to keep it.

Sobadu was one of those people. Cady and Varlo might be as well if they could get someone else to do their dirty work.

◆ ◆ ◆

Angeline awoke the next day and worried about the weaving operation in Gosport. She was encouraged by what had happened Sunday and Monday. With the extra information she and Michael had come by at the Hawke Street Pub, she knew she could bring them down, but she needed the Jamaicans to know that information, so they could rise against Sobadu. Michael could have the Morning Post print the truth about those corrupt men all he wanted, but the Jamaicans wouldn't learn from those printings. Ninety-nine percent of them were illiterate.

She said a private, small prayer of thanks to Abigail Stewart for her insistence that Angeline learn how to read and write. It was soon after that prayer that she came to the decision that she had to risk it all for her mother's memory. She didn't believe in anything called destiny, she just felt like she had to follow through with this and get the Jamaicans to oust Sobadu, even kill him and rid themselves of the scourge he represented.

She quickly jotted down the following to be sent to Agnes and Dana with Jerdan's morning ferry ride back to Gosport.

> *I am staying in Portsmouth until I can find justice for Dominique. I don't know if I will be successful. I may be in danger. If I do not return, God bless you both for helping me when you did. If I do not return, with this note I give you the loom and the weaving business that we have with Haslar Hospital. In the event I do not return, please tell Dr. Williams thank you and notify Dr. Jim Hawkins in Bristol. The house is his if I die.*

It was really hard to write those words: "If I do not return" and "If I die." What had she done? She was up against ruthless men who wouldn't hesitate to kill her to keep their power. Cady, Varlo, Sobadu. She hated these men and the corruption they stood for. No one else was stepping up to stop them. She had to do it. With her royal blood surging to the surface, she picked up her bible, tucked her knife in her belt, and made sure she had her pouch with money and the stash of retaliatory poison. Then she walked to the ferry dock and delivered the note with some money to Jerdan to take to the weaving shed.

It was an unusual week. Tuesday through Friday, she did exactly what she had done on Monday. It was strange yet satisfying. She fully expected to be hassled, heckled, and pulled down from the crates she stood on. But she wasn't. She watched the people who got close to her, half expecting a knife to jut out from a hand. But it didn't happen. She kept her bible in her left hand with her right hand free to reach for her own blade if she had to defend herself.

But as each day wore on, the number of people who stopped and listened to her increased in number. No constables stopped. They tried to ignore her. Maybe Portsmouth was used to having preachers on the sidewalk. But their reasons didn't worry her, she just kept on. It was a monotonous litany to be sure. She'd read a passage of the Christian bible, then shift to talking about wages and workers' rights. She threw in Sobadu's name and blamed him for her mother's death as loud as she could. She didn't stop until after lunch each day, preferring to rest in the afternoons.

Michael had used his influence to get the Morning Post to print more of her story. The "Mysterious Death of Dominique," the headline read. The newspaper did it for their own selfish reasons of course. They could sell papers with headlines that screamed about murder. Angeline didn't care. At least they didn't have to be paid to write and print the story that she was yelling about on the docks. They mentioned her as Dominique's daughter and how she was seeking justice for the death. Even though the blacks wouldn't buy the single sheet tabloid, white people would.

◆ ◆ ◆

Sobadu had held his drums, dance, music, rum, and drugs-for-all Sunday ritual. Sobadu was especially worked up because of the news he had heard earlier in the day from Delroy. Delroy was generally unreliable, but Sobadu thought he had him under his control enough that he wouldn't deliberately tell a lie.

At the end of his rant against the whites and all things English, Sobadu passionately urged his followers to reject all things white—including, white culture, white religion, and white morals.

With the Jamaicans sufficiently intoxicated with salvia-laced rum, he pranced around them in a circle and extolled his own virtues. It was the end of a long-winded diatribe by Sobadu against all things except the power of Obeah. With a nod from Sobadu, the drumbeats that had thumped steadily for the past hour became silent.

"I am the one who keeps you from harm. I, Sobadu, care for you. I give you herbs to soothe your lonely spirit. The English will never help you. They only want to use you, exploit you like they did in Jamaica. You can rely on me! Rely on the power of Obeah!

"You are no longer slaves. You are freemen and women. Yes! Yes! Yes! You can be glad. Now you are free and you can rejoice. Chant loudly with me to celebrate this freedom!"

All the men and women present chanted along with Sobadu. It was an eerie, intoxicated sound that reverberated throughout the warehouse.

Obi-loa- Oh…ANA-LEA-MAH
Obi-loa- Oh…ANA-LEA-MAH
Obi-loa- Oh…ANA-LEA-MAH
Obi-loa- Oh…ANA-LEA-MAH

"I tell you now. Listen to me. Listen to me. Beware. There is a black woman among us. She is Jamaican and she must atone for her sins against Obeah. She has spread lies against Obeah. She has told lies against Sobadu. She says terrible things, false things. As you leave here tonight, remember her name. She is called Angeline. She is no angel from above. She lies. If you see her, I give you the power and the strength of Obeah to harm her. Take her from this earth. If you see her in Buckland, she can be killed, and you will be rewarded. But nowhere else. Obeah is rich and powerful. Obeah will reward you for this. Remember her name—Angeline."

With that final charge, Sobadu nodded to the drummers to continue, and he left with Slash close behind him. He felt smug as he walked the short distance in the dark to Delroy's room where he would spend the night. He had unleashed almost fifty Jamaicans to kill Angeline without retribution. He thought, *I don't have to do this myself. They'll gladly do this for me.*

◆ ◆ ◆

Monday morning, Angeline went back to her preaching spot on the docks. She was surprised to see Noah standing there. The shipyards were a good half mile walk from the docks. What was he doing there?

"You'd better stop, Angeline," said Noah.

"Why? I'm getting more attention every day. People recognize me. The black workers even smile."

"They won't today," said Noah. "You're a marked woman. Last night Sobadu put a bounty on your head at his ritual dance."

"A bounty? What do you mean?"

"He said that if you step foot in Buckland, anyone can kill you and not be punished. They will be rewarded."

"He can't do that!" spat Angeline, only half-convinced that this was a real possibility.

"Yes he can. Since he can get away with anything he wants in his section of this town, he told the Jamaicans to 'take you from this earth.' I know, I was there. He said, 'the power of Obeah is with you to kill Angeline.'"

"Why should I believe you? You're just trying to scare me."

"Yes, I am. But would I be here this early in the morning to tell you if it was a lie?"

"Would the Jamaicans do that?" Angeline was shaken. If it was true, she would have to watch out for every black person in Portsmouth.

"Not everyone would kill for him, but all it takes is one true believer."

Angeline was disturbed. "Noah, I can't quit. I have to tell them that Sobadu is paid to keep their wages low."

It was Noah's turn to be shocked. "What do you mean, 'paid to keep wages low?'"

"I overheard the mayor and a man named Varlo—"

"I know him, he's an alderman."

"Yes. Varlo. They said they paid Sobadu to control the blacks and keep the black laborers' wages down even though they deserved to be paid as much as white laborers."

Noah clenched his jaw and snarled, "The Jamaicans I know would like to hear that the great Obeah man is a thief stealing from all of us."

"Don't you see?" Angeline said. "We have to tell everyone. They'll throw him out."

Noah was certain of what he said next. "No, they would do more than that. Our people have been suffering too long to take this lightly. They would do more than that. Much more."

"I want to tell them all. Can you tell them for me since I can't go into Buckland?"

"Tell them what?" said Noah. "Listen, I have to run to work now."

"Tell them to come here at the docks tonight after the sun goes down for a freedom rally. Yes, that's what I'll call it; a freedom rally. Don't tell them what it's about. That way you won't get into any trouble. At the rally, I'll tell everyone. I'll shout it to the sky. He killed my mother. I have enough cause to have him killed!"

"I can only do so much at the shipyards. It's your funeral if he gets to you first. But if you get something printed, I can have some of my friends post them in Buckland this afternoon."

"But so few of the Jamaicans read," interrupted Angeline.

"That may be true. But the ones who can will pass on the information." With that, Noah turned and walked hurriedly to the shipbuilding area.

◆ ◆ ◆

Delroy knew where Quigley kept his pistol since Quigley had pulled it from below his counter once and threatened him. Stealing the gun would be easy. He knew Quigley kept some of the more exotic poisons out of sight in the rear room of the store. He would get Quigley to fetch them, leaving the counter unattended.

"I need something for Sobadu," said Delroy, looking at Quigley straight in the eye. He knew Quigley barely tolerated him, but had to since Delroy worked for Sobadu.

"What is it?" asked Quigley with a snarl.

"He wants belladonna," said Delroy.

"All right. Just a minute, I keep it in the back. I'll put it on the tab I keep for him. I don't suppose he'd trust you with any money."

Quigley left, and with a quick move, Delroy got the gun, stuffed it in his belt, and pulled his shirt down to conceal it. Delroy left with the drug without another word spoken by either man. He didn't go anywhere near his room. He had other plans. He was very good at sneaking through the streets unnoticed. He could live like that until he had an opportunity to use the gun.

◆ ◆ ◆

Angeline spent another morning at the docks. There were so many people there, her rants must have been heard by some. Angeline spotted Vincent and called out to him. "Vincent come over here! I want to tell you something. It will only take a minute."

Vincent came over to where Angeline was standing. "I can't stay. I have to work."

"Right, Vincent. But tell everyone there will be a torchlight freedom rally tonight right here. After sundown."

"Freedom rally?" asked Vincent. "Freedom from what?"

"Freedom from the oppression of low wages," replied Angeline. "You'll find out more tonight. I'll explain then."

Angeline hopped down from the crate and hurried to the warehouse where Michael was working. She found him directing workers to move bales of cotton onto horse-drawn wagons for shipment to a customer.

"I need some flyers printed as fast as you can get them made. They should read in big letters, *Torchlight Freedom Rally Tonight. The docks*," blurted Angeline.

"Wait just a minute, Angeline. What's going on?" asked Michael, trying to slow her down. "Torchlight Freedom Rally?"

"That's right, but don't come. It's going to be for blacks only. It's getting dangerous. I've just been told that Sobadu has given permission to his Jamaican Obeah followers to kill me if I step foot into his territory in Buckland. You know the white constabulary leaves him alone. You know the mayor pays him off. We have, I mean, I have to tell them before I get killed."

"He's ordered his people to kill you?" said an incredulous Michael.

"That's what I've been told. That's why I need to get my message out and get it out immediately, if not sooner. Tonight is the night. There's no time to waste arguing about it."

"If you butt heads with him, you'll lose. You can't take him on by yourself."

"I won't. If I can get the Jamaicans to turn from him and follow me, I'll have them to back me up."

"Are you insane?"

Angeline was talking about as fast as she could. Noah's message minutes earlier scared her and she knew she had to act.

"I need to get flyers up this afternoon and get them nailed to poles so people come. They need to be printed fast and distributed fast. Can you get them printed? Please. That's all I'm asking you to do. The rest is too dangerous, and it's not your fight. I'll pay for them."

"I can't leave this job. We're way too busy. But let me write a note to the Morning Post. I'll tell them who you are and to do this for you as fast as possible and to bill my dad later. I'm sure he'd take care of the cost. You don't have to."

Michael went to a small desk in the corner of the warehouse, found some paper and a quill and ink, then penned a small note and gave it to Angeline. She took the note and ran to the Morning Post's office. It was a small one-room shop with a printing press.

She gave the editor Michael's note and he immediately called on his typesetter to set type and roll out a hundred sheets with the torchlight rally announcement. Within an hour they were done. When she saw them, Angeline's heart raced as she took the sheets and ran to the shipyards. She decided not to linger there once she arrived. The constables were always looking for her and she had to sneak close enough to see Noah on a small break. She approached him quickly. He took half the leaflets and stuffed them into his crude knapsack.

She took the remaining handbills and ran back to the docks and gave one to any black man who looked interested. "Bring your friends," she said as she handed them out. "Lots of fireworks tonight."

A constable watched her hand out the flyers, came straight up to her, and bracing his musket across her chest, he said, "What exactly are you handing out? I've seen you this past week, yelling from that crate about your mother. Are you trying to incite a riot?"

Angeline didn't want to go to jail, especially with her rally planned for this evening. She decided to tell the biggest lie she could in order to get the policeman to leave her alone. "I was told to hand these out. I needed to make a few pennies, officer. I don't know what any of this is about."

"Who gave them to you?" asked the constable, glancing at the words on the handbill.

"I don't know," answered Angeline, lying as convincingly as she could. "It was this white gentleman, gray hair, about fifty years old. He looked like the mayor."

"So the mayor gave them to you?"

"I can't be sure. He didn't say his name. He just gave me a few pence and asked me to distribute them along the docks."

"I'll take one and find out who's behind this," grumbled the policeman. "I don't need trouble on the docks tonight."

◆ ◆ ◆

John Cady looked at the handbill and then handed it back to the constable. "I know nothing about this. Who gave it to you? Was it a labor agitator? A black man?"

"No sir, it was a young black woman. She's been at the docks last week, spouting bible quotes and yelling about her mother being murdered by Sobadu."

"Sobadu? She used his name?"

"That's right."

"She been saying anything else?"

"Well, she has rambled on about wages for black folks. But I thought she was crazy so I just let her go on. Not too many people were paying attention to her. Well, at least not at first."

"Not at first. You mean more people began to listen to her?" said Cady, the blood in his face turning bright red.

"Yeah, I guess so."

"You idiot. Why didn't you break them up? You have that big musket in your hands. Why didn't you send them and her packing? Now maybe we'll get a full-scale riot on our hands tonight. I'm going to send some of my men there tonight to shut her up. You tell your sergeant about this so he can have men there as well. We have to nip this labor unrest in the bud."

CHAPTER 20

PORTSMOUTH DOCKS

Sobadu wanted Delroy to send a message for him, but he was nowhere to be found. *He's obviously sleeping somewhere,* Sobadu thought. *Lazy good-for-nothing…*

Sobadu got Joel, another one of his guards, to come in. Joel and one other man had been standing guard for the afternoon at Delroy's place, making sure no one would go upstairs to see Sobadu unless he wanted them to.

"Joel, come in here," commanded Sobadu. "I want you to find Slash and bring him in here.

Twenty minutes later when Slash came in, he was carrying a poster that he had ripped off a pole near his boarding room. He gave it to Sobadu without a word. Just the two of them were in the room, so Sobadu felt he could speak freely. *"What's this Torchlight Freedom Rally? Portsmouth Docks?"* Freedom from what?"

Slash never said a word because Sobadu never wanted to hear anybody else's voice but his own.

"Do you know who put these up in Buckland?"

Slash just shook his head.

"I have a feeling I know who did this. Angeline has been barking about me all week. It's time we brought her here and took care of her. Even if she doesn't step foot voluntarily in Buckland, we can still bring her here. If something happens to her, it's under my jurisdiction just as they have told me. Black on black justice—that's what the mayor called it."

Slash nodded his head slowly, smirking while he did it.

Sobadu shared the grin. "I'll have a surprise for her. I'll give her the same poison we gave her mother. It will be undetected, violent, and sure. Go to Baffin pond at dusk when the newts are feeding and mating and grab a few of them. Get back as soon as you can. I'll mix up a drink for her. Then we'll grab her after her rally at the docks and bring her back to the warehouse for a 'very private' final meeting."

Slash left Sobadu and made his way down the stairs and into the streets. He had to walk a mile to Baffin pond to the east where he could capture the small salamanders.

What he didn't know was that Delroy had been hiding in the alleyway nearby, crouching behind a barrel. Delroy had spent the entire afternoon there, watching and waiting. It was what he had done best during his young life. He was not about to let Slash threaten to kill him again. But the problem with Quigley's gun was that it was a small flintlock with only one shot. He didn't have powder or extra shot, so he had to make good on his first and only attempt. He had to shoot close up, since the flintlock was so inaccurate at anything over ten feet away. He couldn't afford to give Slash an opportunity to pull his machete or the knife in a sheath looped around his neck.

When he saw Slash enter the street opposite of where Delroy was hiding, he overheard Slash tell one of the guards that he would be back soon. He was going to the pond to collect something for Sobadu.

At least now Delroy didn't have to duck and cover himself along a myriad of city streets trying to figure out where Slash was going.

Having been to the pond many times as an unpaid slave-carrier of collected herbs and lizards for Sobadu, Delroy knew exactly where to go.

Keeping himself hidden from his quarry, Delroy ran north to

New Road and then east to Tangier road and then to the pond where he could hide. He didn't want to follow Slash. Slash would follow the shorter route on St. Mary's road, then head north to the pond. Delroy had to arrive first. If Slash sensed he was being followed, he would have the upper hand, and if it came to a knife fight, Delroy knew he would be killed.

Delroy's fight tactic was simple. He would run ahead, hide behind a tree near the pond and shoot Slash as he came near.

Late afternoon was turning into dusk. The sun was setting over the Solent as Delroy waited. Since he had run to the pond, his heartrate was elevated. Each minute that went by seemed like an hour. His heart raced, and he tried to calm himself down, taking long deep breaths. It was a warm August night and Delroy's forehead and shirt were damp with sweat. Slash would surely be there soon. Delroy removed the gun from his belt, pulled back on the hammer, and waited.

He listened carefully for any footsteps in the brush. He had to rely on his hearing. If he turned around too soon and Slash was too far away, he would probably miss. He waited and waited. The tension mounted in his trigger finger. Then suddenly, Slash walked past his hiding tree. Quickly, Delroy jumped out from behind the tree, revealing his hiding spot, moved toward Slash, and that very moment Slash heard Delroy's movement. Slash reached for the knife around his neck but he was too late. He was only five feet away when Delroy pulled the trigger and Slash went down backwards, a .40 caliber bullet hole in his chest.

Delroy turned the pistol around and held it by the barrel so he could use it as a club if needed, but it wasn't necessary. Slash didn't move. Delroy reached down and took both the small throwing blade and the machete from Slash's body, and threw the pistol into the reeds. He didn't want to be holding it if the constabulary started asking questions. It was time to get out of there. The loud report from the pistol would draw attention.

He grabbed one of Slash's legs and hauled him to the edge of the weeds at the edge of the pond. Then he put the knives into his belt and ran as fast as he could to the west until he found cover behind a building where he stopped to rest. He shivered from the adrenaline that filled every vein in his body.

He wondered if this was what revenge felt like. Was it satisfaction seeing a tormentor dead? Was it knowing that this assassin was gone? Was it knowing that he would never be treated like a dog nor threatened again by this paid thug? Whatever the true emotion was, it didn't matter, he was alive, and Slash was dead.

Delroy rested awhile, gathered his wits, and then went to the docks. He wanted to see what the Freedom Rally was all about.

◆ ◆ ◆

After the sun set, Angeline went to the docks. When she arrived, Noah was there with a few of his friends. Their torches lit up the night. Michael had followed her there even though she had told him to stay away. He felt a kindship to her rebel nature. Deep down he knew the black workers were right in asking for better pay. But he also knew that Angeline had another motive. If Sobadu had told his followers to kill her, she was in a lot of danger. But strangely she didn't seem to be acting like it. She may have had a knife in her belt, but it wouldn't be enough if a swarm of Jamaicans wanted to end her life. He decided to stay out of sight and watch her speech from the sidelines, keeping an eye out for anyone who might attack her.

To Michael's surprise the crowd grew to almost fifty people; almost all were black. A few women had joined their men at the rally, but only a few.

Angeline stood on top of a wagon at the docks. There were bits of raw cotton but no bales. The evening breeze was coming off the Solent, throwing a rustling wind through the torch flames.

She stood in the center of the wagon and looked out at the crowd. She wished more people were there, but the posters had been distributed only that afternoon. She wanted hundreds to hear her voice. Every day since the Sunday she'd spoken at Wesley's garden sermon, she had felt bolder, stronger, and more confident that she could sway people's thinking with her passion.

She didn't see more than a couple of white faces and those belonged to a couple of tough looking men who stood apart from the blacks. They seemed to be hanging next to a pole for support. Perhaps they just left a pub, saw the handbill, and wanted to know what the ruckus was about.

If it's a ruckus they want, I'll give them one.

Despite having been preaching in the morning and distributing the handbills in the afternoon, Angeline had a burst of energy that flowed from her conviction that Sobadu had to pay for his crime. But she needed the crowd's support. Maybe it would be tonight. Her only back up plan was that she was not going to back away nor back down. Her mother's life had to be avenged.

In her loudest voice, Angeline started talking. "My name is Angeline. Some of you know me. Most of you have seen me at the shipyards or down here at the docks preaching the Christian word. Well, I have read the Old Testament too."

Angeline picked up her bible and read:

"In Deuteronomy it says: *God says It is mine to avenge; I will repay. In due time their foot will slip; their day of disaster is near and their doom rushes upon them.*"

Angeline yelled out as loud as she could, "You know whose doom it is. It is Sobadu's! Deuteronomy also says: *But if there is any further injury, then you shall appoint as a penalty life for life, eye for eye, tooth for tooth…* Well he has taken the life of my mother. And he will pay for it. We have God on our side. He said: *Rejoice, O nations, with His people; For He will avenge the blood of His servants, and will render vengeance on His adversaries.*

"I, Angeline, will have my vengeance!"

Angeline put the bible down and continued at full voice, "I didn't just bring a bible tonight. I brought the truth. What is that truth? The truth is that Sobadu had my mother killed. He collected poison from the hearts and livers of toads and newts and dipped that poison into candle wicks which burned while my mother slept. The poison filled the air in her room and suffocated her. It was a horrible death.

"He tries to fill your stomachs with poison too. He does this to make you believe he is a magic Obeah man who will cure all your troubles. But has he? Ask yourselves, does all his rubbish make your lives better, even after you were made free men and free women? It only makes you soft and compliant to his wishes, not yours. Are you free? Are you? Or are you a slave to him?"

Angeline saw the receptive looks on the faces of people who seemed to be listening to her. The crowd size seemed to grow, so Angeline increased her rage.

"Sobadu not only killed my mother, he killed my father too. My father Tacky was of royal chieftain Ashanti blood. Yet in Jamaica he was a slave. My father led a rebellion when I was just five years old. My mother wrote me a letter the day before she died which said that Sobadu sprinkled phony magic dust on Tacky and his men so they would think they were safe from the guns of the plantation owners. It was a fraud. They all perished. When my father and the remainder of his African-Jamaican rebels ran to the hills, the coward Sobadu told the chasing maroon and British soldiers where Tacky was hiding. He was shot and killed. Sobadu escaped to England after drugging the slaves on the boat and did the same when you all came here."

Many of the Jamaicans looked at each other in amazement. They seemed to be asking themselves if what they were hearing could be true—if they really had been duped by a massive manipulator.

"But way beyond his past crimes—which he must atone for—is his present crime. You are paid only half of what the whites are paid. Is that not right? Answer me. Is that not right?"

Ten or twelve men spoke up, one after another: "That's right, half of what the whites get. We should be paid what they are paid! We want more. We deserve more!"

One man gathering up some 'mob courage started a loud chant: "Paid the same."

Others picked up the chant. Angeline encouraged them and cried out, "Say it again. Paid the same! Paid the same!"

The crowd was revving up. "Paid the same," they yelled.

"Do you know why you are not paid the same? Do you know why?"

The crowd kept chanting, "Paid the same." They were in tune with her now, and the feeling was intoxicating.

She raised her voice ever louder. "Do you want to know why?"

The crowd responded. "Why?!"

"Move in closer, and I'll tell you why."

The crowd jostled one another to hear what she had to say next.

As the crowd moved closer, the two white thugs holding up the pole were whispering to each other trying to decide whether or not to challenge the speaker and knock her off the wagon. One was completely against this simply because the crowd of black workers was getting larger and more willful. They were supporting her and there were only two of them against what seemed like a crowd of sixty to seventy now.

Delroy had been listening and paying attention. His mind was a dizzying combination of regret for having listened to a fraud like Sobadu and the realization that if Sobadu found out he had killed Slash, that his life would be over.

He had to take sides now. If he joined this young woman, and she had the crowd with her, he might be safe. If he went back and told Sobadu what was happening, Sobadu might kill him on the spot. His decision was made. He was tired of being scared by Sobadu. He was tired of being treated like a mangy street cur. He made his way to the side of the wagon and waited. He was good at waiting and finding the right moment when he was needed.

Angeline didn't know where her power to incite the crowd came from. As the crowd moved closer to her, she thought of her father Tacky back in Jamaica, tired of being whipped and driven like a mule in the sugar cane fields. She thought of him harnessing his anger, urging two hundred men to risk their lives to follow him and rebel against the plantation owners. It was a bloody rebellion which ended in his death, but he died like the noble he was.

Angeline caught her momentum and yelled, "I have the truth. I overheard two people talking. One was the mayor, the other was an alderman named Varlo."

Someone yelled out from the crowd, "He's on the city council."

Someone else yelled, "The mayor's name is Cady."

Angeline continued. "They were talking about Sobadu and how they paid him every year to 'keep you in line' and make sure you didn't strike or demand higher wages."

A number of people yelled, "Paid him? What? Paid him to keep our wages low?"

Angeline said, "That's right. You were freed by the Mansfield decision over two and a half months ago. You are no longer slaves and yet if you drink his drug-laced rum, you will be a slave to whatever he commands you to do. He is paid by the city government to keep you in your place. Do you accept that!?" Angeline yelled it again. "Do you accept that?"

A voice came from the crowd, a voice of dissention. "How do we know you're telling the truth? You might be making this up."

Angeline was silent for a moment. "I heard them talking," she finally blurted out.

Delroy knew he had to say something. He knew too much to keep quiet. He hopped up on the wagon, and although Angeline was startled and started to reach for her knife, Delroy ignored her and spoke to the crowd.

"My name is Delroy and I have been working for Sobadu for the past five years. Many of you know me. You have seen me deliver messages for Sobadu all over Buckland and elsewhere. Everything this woman says is true. I have been in the room with him when he has sneered at you for being stupid. Laughed that you have been so gullible. Bragged how he could get you to behave while he pocketed the money the city gave him."

"What can we do?" someone in the crowd yelled.

"Tomorrow you should strike!" said Angeline. "Noah, I know you're out there. Will you lead them?"

Noah shouted back, "Shipyards or docks?"

Angeline answered immediately, the fervor in the crowd had to be maintained. "The shipyards where you work."

"The shipyards it is." Noah turned around and shouted, "We'll need every single one of you. Without fail. Angeline, I will lead if you are by my side."

"All right, tomorrow is a strike," yelled Angeline. "Tonight, we need to get Sobadu."

Delroy came up with a plan on the spot. "Everyone go to the warehouse where you have your Sunday meetings. Hide in the dark. I will bring Sobadu to you. Be prepared to take him captive. He won't surrender easily."

Angeline sensing the plan immediately yelled, "Go everyone. Douse your torches and go."

She turned to face Delroy. "Can you get him there?"

"Yes, I can do that," replied Delroy. "It may mean my life, but I can bring him. I've just now figured out a way to get him there."

It wasn't until the crowd started to move that she took stock of what she had for the upcoming confrontation. She had her crystal for good luck, her blade in case she had to defend herself, and the pouch containing the pufferfish poison.

As she came down from the wagon, Michael ran up to her. "I saw two of Varlo's men watching the entire preceding. They started to make a move towards you but thought better of it. They're probably going to tell Cady what they heard. Let me be your bodyguard on the way to the warehouse."

"Yes, Michael. Thanks, and thanks to you for all you've done. This is far from over."

The two of them walked with a small group of the black laborers who had listened to Angeline. There was some strength in numbers and Varlo's men stayed at a distance and never tried to attack them.

As they walked, Angeline made a decision. It wasn't easy given all that Michael had done for her, but if there was to be a problem with the constabulary, Angeline didn't want Michael mixed up in it.

"Michael, when we get to the warehouse, I want you to go home and stay there. I won't be staying there with you and your father anymore."

"What are you talking about?"

"Didn't you hear their reaction to my speech? They want me to lead them."

Michael shook his head. "It's a fantasy. You're dreaming this up."

"No, I'm not. And I'm serious about you not going into the warehouse. I have to do what I have to do. I'll contact you later in the week. Go home tonight. Go to your job in the morning. Your father needs you."

"Why should I listen to a crazed woman who's two years younger than I am? Tell me. Who are you?"

"You forget one thing. I am the daughter of an African Chieftain. I am Tacky's daughter."

◆ ◆ ◆

Delroy walked to his room in Buckland. He didn't want to get there too quickly. He wanted the Jamaicans who had been at the rally to get to the warehouse and hide before he brought Sobadu there.

After passing through the two guards at his residence, he got permission to see Sobadu.

"Where's Slash?" Sobadu commanded. He was as angry as Delroy had ever seen him.

"He sent me to tell you he has Angeline."

"Where!?" Sobadu yelled half angry and half excited that he could put an end to the woman yelling his name in the city streets.

"He has her in the warehouse, ready for you to take care of her. He would have done it, but he knew you wanted the pleasure."

"And I do," said Sobadu as he gathered up his newt poison and followed Delroy down the stairs and into the streets toward the warehouse. It was only a few blocks away and they would get there in five minutes or less.

Delroy was standing in the doorway and Sobadu roughly elbowed him aside as he stormed out the door. He had all he needed. He would shove the newt poison in Angeline's nostrils and she could inhale it until she choked and died. He had heard enough of her talk about him murdering her mother and father. It was time to act and finish her. She was in his territory; he could do as he liked.

◆ ◆ ◆

In the warehouse, most of the Jamaicans had hidden themselves against the walls and behind bales of cotton and tobacco. They tried to stay quiet. Noah and five others perched near the door. They didn't want Sobadu to put up much of a fight, so they decided to tackle him and pin him down with overwhelming force. Noah had a club in his hand ready to convince Sobadu, the big man, to stay down.

Angeline stood alone in the middle of the room, a single torch at her feet slowly burning itself out. She was the bait to draw Sobadu into the room and towards her. It was the perfect trap.

Sobadu rushed to the warehouse and entered through the back door as he was expected to. The moment he saw Angeline, he took three more eventful steps toward the torch-lit woman who was causing him so much grief.

When he first saw her, his anger ruled his thoughts. Then an instant later, he asked himself, *Where is Slash*? He didn't see him standing next to Angeline.

In that instant, five men tackled Sobadu, and brought him to the ground on his stomach. He thrashed as best he could, but a fifty-year-old man could not possibly overpower five young Jamaicans who wanted to kill him. One held his right hand, one his left, one was kneeling on his back, and the other two knelt on the back of each of his calves. He winced in pain from the pressure. As he struggled, he was able to release one arm from the grasp of the man who held it. When Noah saw that, he stepped in and belted Sobadu on the back of his head as hard as he could with the club. Sobadu went limp.

When he was unconscious, three men tied his legs together and stretched the rope around his neck and then to his hands tied behind his back. They stuffed a rag into his mouth so he couldn't speak. He couldn't continue the fight once he was conscious without strangling himself.

When he woke a few moments later, he was tipped on his side. He was surrounded by Jamaicans whom he had once commanded, manipulated, and duped into thinking he was an Obeah man who had magical powers over them. They were now convinced that he had done all of this to enrich himself with money and power for his own selfish ends.

Angeline stood by him and spoke the final words he would hear. "Hold his head," she ordered. Three of the men gripped his head, holding it still.

"You killed my father with your treachery, Sobadu. You killed my mother with your newt poison. I want you to know that the last voice you hear will be from their daughter as she pours the same pufferfish poison in your ear."

Angeline took the poison from her pouch, opened the vial, and put the pufferfish poison directly into his ear.

He tried to thrash but he couldn't move his head or his body.

Within minutes his breathing became labored, his face turned red, he started sweating, and then was paralyzed. He tried to shout through the gag but couldn't. The seizure stopped his heart within a few minutes.

Angeline rose. She had accomplished what she had set out to do. The only emotion she felt was the deep satisfaction of taking down this murderer. She had no regrets about killing him.

However, she knew that her mission wouldn't end with Sobadu's death. She had gained the confidence of the Jamaicans and realized they depended on her to lead. They needed higher wages and she was not afraid to help them demand the wages they deserved.

There was a silent mood in the room that she needed to change. She raised her voice in triumph. "Everyone who is here, look upon the death of this tyrant and rejoice! You are not in his chains any longer. But your struggles are just beginning. Tomorrow morning meet me at the shipyards at dawn. Noah and I will lead you. Tomorrow we will demand higher wages. Tomorrow we strike!"

ABOUT THE AUTHOR

RICHARD A. YACH takes great pride in creating "Angeline" for his readers. He has strong attachments to the characters he has created in this novel and others including "The Destiny of Jim Hawkins", "For the Love of Livian", and "Raven's Revenge".

As a corporate trainer, he has produced and published over 300 training videos, manuals and technical magazine articles. He has also written five plays, four of which have been produced. These include One Way, Brave New World Revisited, The Bard of Beale Street, A Round with the Boys; Golf is a Four-Letter Joke, and Daggett, Dag-Nabbit! Richard lives with his wife Linda in West Des Moines, Iowa with children and grandchildren in the Midwest and California.